Skiptrace

Skiptrace

Antoinette Azolakov

BANNED BOOKS
Austin, Texas

LIBRARY OF CONGRESS
Library of Congress Cataloging-in-Publication Data

Azolakov, Antoinette, 1944–
    Skiptrace / Antoinette Azolakov.—1st ed.
    p. cm.
ISBN 0-934411-09-3

    I. Title.
PS3551.Z66S58   1988
813'.54—dc19
                                88-967
                                 CIP

For our courage,
our beauty,
our laughter,
and our strength,
this book is dedicated
to all lesbians.

———

ACKNOWLEDGMENTS: Although everybody I've ever known helped make *Skiptrace* possible, I want to say a special thank you to Anne Peticolas for encouraging me to write it, to Lisa Carrie Brown for reopening long-locked doors, and to Frances M. Elliott for her enthusiastic support.

... AND A SPECIAL NOTE: When I was very young and my name was Elizabeth Ann Holland, I lost touch with a woman I loved. Claudia, if you read this, write to me in care of Banned Books.

—Antoinette Azolakov

CHAPTER 1

B y three o'clock Tuesday afternoon, the thermometer stood at one hundred and two degrees. It would probably climb another degree or two in the next hour. Par for the course for July. Sweat trickled down my face and neck, soaking my shirt around the collar, and the blinding glare, when I looked out from under the live oaks, made my eyes seem to vibrate in my skull.

Not even a leaf stirred in the big trees. Among the little group of women standing in the shade no one stirred much, either, except to rustle the dry grass with a shifting foot now and then.

Six blue-and-white Austin police cars were parked haphazardly along the street and in the driveways of neighboring houses, leaving room for the big, white van with the logo of the Travis County Medical Examiner to back into Sandy Marigold's driveway. It sat there now, as it had for what seemed like hours, while radios squawked unintelligibly from the cop cars and men in navy blue police uniforms so dark they looked black in the sun now and then moved in and out of the front door and around the sides and back of Sandy's house. Finally two men in suits came out of the door and walked over to where we stood.

"Okay, ladies, we're going to have a lot of work to do here and it'll take a while, so why don't we just get your names and you can all go on home."

Women shuffled their feet.

"Why do you need our names?" I wanted to know.

"It's just standard procedure." It was the older of the two detectives, I assumed, who did the talking. His tone was reasonable, even casual, as though any group of dykes should think nothing of giving their names to the police.

I wasn't buying it. "We're not witnesses, officer. We got here after you did."

"Nothing to worry about. We understand you knew the victim, and we may need your help, that's all."

"But. . . ."

"So if you'll just give your names to Sgt. Harris, here, you can all go someplace cool for a while. Nothing else is going to happen here."

"Well, how will we know what you find out? I mean, she was our friend, and—"

"We'll be talking to you. Or if you have anything important, call us," he said, and he walked off.

"Name?" said Sgt. Harris to the nearest woman, and he started writing in a notebook. It didn't take long to get us all recorded and establish that none of us knew anything to warrant taking us in to make statements. The only effect I could see of his taking our names was that now he had six of us on a list of Dykes at the Scene of the Crime.

Just about the time Harris was closing his book, there was movement at the door of the house, and the two people who'd arrived in the van came out, not hurrying, maneuvering a wheeled stretcher over the threshold and onto the concrete walk. On the stretcher lay a lumpy plastic sack. They got the cart to the back of the van and shoved it in, the wheeled legs folding with a bump as it slid inside. The two technicians closed the van's back doors and one laughed at some remark the other made. They went around to the front and got in. No need for anybody to ride in the back with Sandy. When her lover had come by to take her out for ice cream, she'd found

her already stiff, and every fly in the neighborhood had
had time to buzz in after all that blood.

As we drifted back toward our cars, Lisa Grantly fell
into step with me.

"I tried to call Dean at his office, but he wasn't there.
I left a message on his machine to call me. God, I hope
he doesn't hear about it on the radio or something first."

"He might. I bet it's on the radio by now."

"But if he's out working on a case or something, he
might not hear it. Sandy mentioned he had some big divorce case he was working on."

I grunted. The thought of a private detective spying
on somebody in a divorce case was unpleasant, and I
felt uneasy, anyway, because of some recent dealings I'd
had with this particular private eye, even if he was a
friend of a dyke I knew. A dead dyke, now.

"He was really crazy about Sandy. It's going to be a
shock," Lisa said.

"Yeah."

We walked on in silence. Then I said, "Listen, Lisa,
will you call me if Dean calls you?"

"Sure. Why?"

"Well. . . ." I hesitated. "I, ah, I just hired him to
do a little work for me."

"Oh." She looked at me curiously. "I'll call you if I
hear from him."

I found a grocery receipt in my billfold and wrote
my phone number on the back. When I handed it to her
she was looking at me curiously, but she was too polite
to ask what work I'd hired Dean Caney for. I didn't want
to tell her, but she was being so considerate about it that
I found myself feeling like I had to. Her silence was more
effective than asking me would have been.

"You know what skiptracing is?" I said. "Where they
check around all over the country to find somebody that's
missing?" She nodded. "Well, I had an old friend—
actually, she was my first lover—and I've lost track of
her over the years, and I hired Dean to run a skiptrace
on her so we could get back in touch. I didn't have any

idea how to do it myself or I would have. I really do prefer to skin my own skunks. But I thought, 'This guy is friendly with dykes, so it ought to be all right.' "

"Uh-huh."

"I never would have gone to just anybody with it. But he was a friend of Sandy's—"

"Take it easy, Cass. I don't see anything wrong with that." She smiled at me, the first smile I'd seen on any of us since I got there.

I smiled back, a little. "Well. So anyway, that's why I wanted to know."

I wasn't telling Lisa, a woman I hardly knew at all, about all the reasons I'd hired Dean to look for Claudia.

We got to my truck and stopped.

"I guess people will be getting together sometime this evening?" I said.

"Yeah, probably at Susan's." Susan lived one street over, on the block behind Sandy's house. It was a common gathering place for the set of women Susan and Sandy and Lisa were part of. I'd been to a party or two there myself.

"I'll probably see you there, then," I told Lisa. "I've got to get back to the job." I climbed into the Chevy's cab and stuck my key into the ignition. "Thanks for stopping by and telling me, Lisa." I'd been out on a job site with my landscaping crew when Lisa had seen my truck and stopped to tell me what had happened to Sandy Marigold. Lisa was free during the day a lot of the time because she worked rotating shifts at a plastics factory. I'd seen her around the bar a lot at night, too, when she was off those hours. She was young, in her twenties, I figured, and could keep up the pace. I'm thirty-eight. I need my rest.

I leaned out the truck window and gave her a kiss, friend to friend. Her arm went around my neck and I got my arm out the window and hugged her, too. We held each other hard for a minute, thinking of what had happened to one of our own. Then she gave me an extra

4

squeeze and walked off toward her car. I started the truck and pulled out.

I was almost at the corner when I glanced in my rear view mirror and saw that two women I didn't know had stopped Lisa and were talking to her. Straight women from the neighborhood? I suddenly didn't want Lisa to have to deal with these strangers about the murder of her friend. I put the truck in reverse and stepped on the gas.

As I backed toward them, they all looked around and I saw a look of acute distress on Lisa's face. I hopped out and walked over.

"Cass," Lisa said as I came up. These are neighbors of Sandy's."

"We live right over there," said one of the women, pointing out two adjacent houses across the street.

"This is Cass Milam," Lisa said. "Tell her what you told me."

The one in the white shorts and the flowered top spoke. "We were just wondering what had happened —all the police and everything—and she told us. We're so sorry about your friend. It's just awful! It must be terrible for you. I know she had a lot of friends. She must have been a nice person."

I nodded, my lips pressed together. I can face nearly anything calmly until somebody sympathizes, and then I want to cry. Hearing them talk about Sandy like that made the fact of her death, the horror and the finality of it, come home to me for the first time. I found I was fighting back tears.

"We, you know, wondered if we should say anything," the woman went on. But it was just so strange, the way he looked when he came out of there earlier, sort of hurrying and looking all around, you know, and so when the police came just a little bit after that girl went in there—"

"Wait a minute," I said. "Who is this 'he' you're talking about?"

5

"Why, that man that lived next door to her. Mr. . . . ." She looked blankly at her friend.

"Cane, or something like that? I didn't know him very well."

"Yes. Mr. Cane. We were sitting there where we were looking out my picture window, and we saw Mr. Cane —is that it? It doesn't seem quite right."

"Caney," I said in a small voice.

"That's it. Caney. I knew 'Cane' wasn't quite right. We saw him come out of there this morning, looking like he was scared or something. He was sure looking around a lot, anyway, like he wondered if anybody was watching."

"Then what did he do?" I said.

"Drove off in his car," said the woman in white shorts.

"No, he didn't," her friend said. "He went back in his house first."

"But he drove off pretty soon, though."

"Yeah, and he was in a hurry."

"Late for work, we thought. I don't know where he worked."

"I do," I said.

"Well, he was over there all the time. He must have had a nice job, if he could take that much time off. He'd be over there in the daytime just about any time that poor girl was home. Was he her boyfriend?"

"I think you'd better go over and tell the police this," Lisa said.

"Oh! Do you really think so? Because we don't want to get anybody in trouble. . . ."

"I'm sure they'd want to know."

"Well, if you think so. . . ."

They started toward Sandy's house and we watched them cross the street and go up to the cop at the front door. He left them there and went inside, and then the two detectives came out and we could see the women talking to them. We were too far away to hear what they said, but the cops were sure listening.

6

Lisa said, disbelievingly, "So Dean did it?"

"Lord, who knows? But it doesn't look good, does it."

"No. It doesn't look good."

I thought about Dean Caney, brawny and tall, but with sensitive, dark eyes and a quiet voice, a man who hung around with lesbians but who always stayed in the background and out of the conversation. A nice guy, 'sweet,' Sandy had called him when she was recommending him to me. A quiet, nice guy who might have beaten in his dyke friend's skull this morning. The quiet man I'd hired to find my long-lost lover.

CHAPTER 2

The traffic was already picking up for the afternoon rush, and I knew better than to go by Ben White Boulevard to get back to the south Austin place where I'd left my crew of two installing landscaping timbers to make some raised flower beds. Ben White is busy most of the day, and rush hours are impossible. I went down Bannister and cut across on Redd Steet. When I got to the client's place, I could see right away that progress had been made. The timbers were all in place and Larry, our teenage summer helper, was pounding in the re-bar stakes to lock them together. One bed already had the stakes in it, and Cheryll, my permanent employee, was shoveling dirt into it from the back of my other truck, the dual-wheeled 'dooley' we used to haul heavy loads.

I climbed out of the truck and Cheryll stopped work and walked over.

"So what happened?"

"Somebody beat Sandy to death. Beat her head in."

"Shit."

"Yeah. Donna found her."

"Shit, how awful."

"Yeah. She was stiff already. In a pool of blood."

Cheryll closed her eyes and made a face. "Who did it, do they know?"

"Maybe Dean. You know, Dean Caney."

"Oh, hell. Why? I mean, why do they think so? Do they have him?"

8

"No. Some neighbors saw him run out of there this morning, though."

"God. Why would he do it? The way he hung around, I thought he was in love with her or something."

"I don't know. Maybe it's frustrating, being in love with a dyke, if you're not one."

"Sometimes it is even if you are one."

"No kidding. Anyway, Lucia might know something about it. She was Sandy's best friend, I think."

"Yeah. Well, maybe we'll know more by tonight. I think probably a bunch of people are getting together at Susan's, Lisa said. Look, why don't y'all knock off for the day? I'm feeling kind of shell-shocked. I'm going home."

"I could stand a beer, myself." Cheryll glanced over at Larry, industriously pounding away with the sledge hammer. "This kid about runs me into the ground."

"Yeah. Me, too." I left the crew of Milam Lawn and Landscape to clean up and headed for Hank Street.

The nice thing about my little house on Hank Street is it's mine—or mine and the mortgage company's. It's small, it's not air-conditioned, and it's not in a classy neighborhood, but I love it. To me and Pamela and Chip, my cats, and Ronson, my Chesapeake Bay retriever, it's home. I pulled into the driveway and ran the truck all the way to the back by the garage to give Cheryll room to park the dooley behind it when she brought it back to exchange for her car, which was parked in front at the curb. I opened the back yard gate, thinking as I did that my chainlink fence suited me better than a cedar privacy one would have because it let the breeze, if any, into my yard. Ronson came bounding up, grinning in his doggy way, and I gave him a good scratch behind the ears. Chip, the orange-striped male cat, came yawning and stretching off the flat roof of the doghouse across the yard and walked to meet me, tail straight up. I had to look around for a minute before I spotted Pamela curled up in a lawn chair. She raised her head, looked at me briefly, and

9

tucked herself firmly into a coil again. She never lowered herself to come to the gate.

Seeing my animals, my house, and my yard all looking so natural and peaceful was a help. I was feeling pretty shaken by the events of the afternoon. I unlocked the back door and went in through the kitchen, remarking to Chip, who had followed me in, that at least there were no dead bodies on the floor. I got a cold beer out of the refrigerator, twisted the top off, and took a gulp as I headed into the bathroom. In the shower I stood a while, just letting the water wash over my head and face, feeling it wash away the tension in my body. After a bit I soaped and rinsed and got out, feeling better.

I was determined not to think of Sandy or Dean right then, so every time an image from the afternoon popped into my mind I shoved it back down and thought of something else, like how good the beer tasted or how cool and hard the floor tiles felt to my tired feet. I'm not a delicate thing, and if I'm not as thin and dainty as the American ideal and the advertisers tell me I ought to be, I still enjoy my body's strength and the work it can do in the Texas sun. So I thought about that and the rough towel rubbing my skin and pushed the murdered woman I'd known to the back of my mind until I'd dressed in cutoff jeans and a tee shirt and had taken my beer with me to the back yard. There I sat in a lawn chair and put my feet up on a stump, took a deep breath, and started confronting the events of the day.

It didn't take long to get from sorrow and horror over the murder of a woman I'd known, to worry over the guy who it looked like must have done it. If he had, and I hoped to god he hadn't, then we had a dyke killer on the loose, and this killer had all the information I could give him about a woman I cared about. What if he'd found her already and turned her into victim number two? But that was silly. Why would he want to kill Claudia, a woman he didn't even know? For that matter, why would he want to kill Sandy Marigold, a woman he not only knew but reportedly cared about?

10

Maybe, I thought for a sweet moment, the cops already have him. If I went in and called the police station, as the detective whose name I didn't know had told us we could do, they might tell me that the case was solved. I heaved myself out of the chair and went in to call.

I got transferred to two different lines before I got Sgt. Harris, who carefully took down my name and address all over again and then told me they had "no suspect in custody at this time."

"What about the guy those two neighbor women told you about?"

"We're following several leads in the case."

"Have you even found Caney to talk to him?"

"The case is under investigation, miss."

"Thank you," I said. He hung up.

I stood there with the phone humming a dial tone at me, then took it up on its offer and dialed Jacko.

If I have a best friend in the world, Jacko — Jaqueline, to her parents — is it. We're as unlike as a pea and a bean in a pod, but we get along. I think our differences actually help. She's learned over the years that I'm never going to approve of her conservative politics or her lust for straight women, and I've learned she's never going to like my uncloseted dykiness and about a hundred other things about me. What keeps us friends is a shared sense of humor and a respect for each other's integrity and a willingness to fight, although in different ways, for what we believe is right. Also we like to go to bed together now and then, and it's a no-hassles and no-hangups situation. That's a big area of agreement.

The phone rang a couple of times before Jacko grabbed it, indicating that she must have been really busy with something else. Most of the time she gets it before the first ring is finished, because she has three phones in a one-bedroom apartment and they're all on long cords so she can drag them to wherever she is at the moment. They're a legacy from an old lover of hers who worked in sales for the phone company. One of those people who, when you apply for phone service, tries at great length

11

to sell you on a setup that would do the White House proud. Of course, it suited Jacko, because she gave her phone number to every new feminine woman she met, and a lot of them called her.

"Jacko," I said.

"Well, hey, lady!" (Even I am a lady to Jacko.) "What you been doing?"

I told her.

"Holy cow! And so, what happened? Who did it? Do they know?"

"Remember Dean Caney? The private eye?"

Jacko did, but not until I prodded her memory. "And Sandy was, let me see, she was the one who used to go with what-was-her-name, that real cute little Spanish girl."

I didn't bother to correct her calling that very politically-active Chicana Sandy used to go with a 'little Spanish girl,' because that was one of the areas we'd agreed to disagree on. I couldn't fight everybody's linguistic battles with Jacko. I had a tough enough time with my own.

"But I thought Sandy and Dean were good friends."

"So did we all. Of course we don't know he did it."

"Well. I'm fixing Hamburger Helper. Come over for supper. You sound like you need company."

She said it in her no-nonsense voice, and I agreed. I could tell I was going to be fussed over, and by then I didn't mind the idea. Every time I told somebody about Sandy it got harder, and I was getting to where I could see the scene in her kitchen in my mind like a too-gory horror film. I was sure it would have been much worse if I'd actually seen it—I felt a stab of deep grief for poor Donna, who had—but my vivid imagination was rapidly supplying more and more sickening details. I could stand a little of Jacko's mothering.

I hung up and finished my beer, called the cats in and fed them, and then walked around the house checking the latches on the screens and the lock on the front door. The thought that a man who knew me might be a killer was making me nervous.

12

The screens wouldn't keep out a ten-year-old child who wanted to get in, I realized, but I had to leave the windows up or the cats would suffocate in the heat. I wondered about getting some kind of window locks that would hold the sashes open a little, just enough to let in some air but no burglars. Or murderers. I left the outside lights and the living room lamp burning and the attic fan on, gathered up Ronson's leash and a rawhide chewbone, stuck my billfold in my hip pocket, and zipped out the back door. Then I zipped back in again to put on my shoes and socks—I was more nervous than I'd thought, apparently—and then I remembered I hadn't checked my mail.

I opened the front door and reached around for the lid of the mailbox to pull out the sheaf of ads and circulars, and as I glanced up, I saw a dark blue Ford sedan speed up and shoot down the street. It had been going quite slowly until I opened the door, or that was the impression I got, the definite impression that the car accelerated when the driver saw me come out. I knew one person who drove a dark blue ford. Dean Caney.

I locked up again, very quickly, and sat down in my living room chair. My heart was beating ninety-to-nothing.

"Stupid," I told myself. "It was not him." And why in the devil would it be, after all? Dean Caney didn't have anything against me, did he? I hardly knew him, did I? I was a client of his, that's all. I didn't even know Sandy that well. All I'd done with Dean Caney was give him money, his retainer for running a skiptrace on Claudia. And besides, he wouldn't be out driving around Austin with the cops looking for him, would he? "It wasn't him, stupid," I said aloud.

Should I call Sgt. Harris and tell him about this? Or would he just think I was a hysterical fool? I went to the phone in the hall and got out the phone book again. This time I wrote the police administrative number on the notepad I keep under the phone. I might need it again, at this rate.

13

I dialed, asked for the extension I'd learned last time, and got not the ever-helpful Sgt. Harris, but someone named Sgt. Alcorn instead. I wondered if he was the older man who'd been at Sandy's.

"Maybe this is nothing," I told him after I identified myself, "but what looked like Dean Caney's car just went by my house."

"You're this..," he paused, and I could hear the noise paper makes when you shuffle several sheets around, "Cassandra Milam? 1406 Hank Street?"

"That's right." At least this guy seemed on top of it.

"And what makes you think this car was the Caney guy? You get a good look at him?"

"No. But this car seemed to be going real slow until I opened the front door and then it speeded up a lot. And the driver could have been Caney. I only saw him out of the corner of my eye."

"Right. Okay, Cassandra, are you going to be there a while?"

"Well, I can be. I was just going out."

"Go on. We'll send a car to check it out, but he's out of the area by now, if it was him. I wouldn't worry about it if I were you. We're pretty sure he's long gone."

"Why? Have you found out anything else?"

He was not to be drawn. "The case is under investigation," he said.

We hung up, and I could picture him saying to one of the other cops something like, "Just a hysterical dyke who's seeing boogers."

I put Ronson in the cab of the dooley, which Cheryll had left in the driveway while I was in the shower, and headed for Jacko's. As I was stopping at the intersection at the end of the block a police car cruised slowly around the corner and idled up Hank, the two cops looking around at the houses as they went. Sgt. Alcorn was a man of his word. Of course, as he had predicted, there was no sign of Dean Caney or his dark blue Ford.

14

CHAPTER 3

The evening with Jacko was a sweet interlude in a day otherwise grim. She'd fussed over me, fed me, talked about things refreshingly different from murder and murderers, and finally taken me to bed. I got home feeling relaxed and peaceful, and the day's events seemed far away and a little unreal.

I was in the shower regretfully washing off the lovely, musky scent of Jacko when the phone rang. It slapped me right back into the tension I'd thought I was rid of. I swore, not because I was going to drip all over the floor when I went to answer it, but because my instant reaction to the phone bell had been to jump six inches. I grabbed a towel and splashed into the hall.

"Cass?" It was Lisa Grantly. "I talked to the police and they wouldn't tell me a thing."

"Yeah, Lisa, I talked to them a couple of times myself."

"And nobody's heard from Dean."

If you don't count my little experience this afternoon, I thought, but I didn't want to go into it again. I was tired, and all I could think of suddenly was how nice the sheets were going to feel to my naked body in about two minutes if I could get Lisa off the phone. I glanced at my watch. It was midnight.

"Yeah, well, I don't know anything I didn't know when I saw you," I told her.

"Yeah. . . . I did find out that they haven't found the weapon."

"Do they know what it was?"

"Something like a piece of pipe or a tire tool, they said."

"Oh. So the killer probably brought it with him and took it away again."

"Yes. I guess he planned to kill her when he came over.

"In cold blood."

"Yeah." She was quiet for a minute. "Somebody killed her in cold blood." Her voice started to shake. "Somebody just kept coldly hitting her and hitting her until she was dead."

"Lisa," I told her, "take it easy." I heard her start to cry. "Just take a deep breath, babe—"

"And they killed her. For nothing. She didn't have anything in the house worth stealing. Just for nothing!"

"Babe, take it easy."

"Oh, Cass, why did he do it? She loved Dean. They were friends. Why? How *could* he?"

"Lisa, baby—"

"Oh, Cass, I—" She broke off, drew a big, shaky breath, and said, "Cass *why* weren't you at Susan's tonight?"

"Huh?" I replied gracefully.

"Well, I mean you said you'd be there, and when you didn't get there at first, I waited and waited, and hell, Cass, I—I wanted to see you."

"See me?" This wasn't sinking in very well.

"Oh, hell, I never intended to do this over the phone. I wanted to see you, woman, because I like you. You know, *like* you? As in find you madly attractive and handsome, etcetera, etcetera?"

"Holy cow. You do?"

"Yes."

"Well, I'll be damned. You do?"

"Yes. Yes! I do!"

16

"Well, I'll be damned."

"You said that."

I thought about Lisa, how her eyes were blue and gentle-looking and her hair was dark, and how she and I had hugged each other through the window of my truck and how she was being so open with me in her feelings about her dead friend, and I said, "I do you, too."

"You do?"

"Have we just traded lines here, or what?"

She laughed, and so did I. "I would never have guessed it," I told her. "I would have thought I was too politically incorrect for you or something."

"Politics ain't everything."

"And too old, too."

"Cass, how old do you think I am?"

"I don't know. About twenty-eight?"

"Thirty-two. So you're just six years older than me, and that's nothing, woman."

So Lisa'd been checking up on me enough even to know my age. "Well," I said. "I'll be damned."

Lisa said, "You said that."

We giggled.

When we finally hung up it was five past one. I was weaving on my feet with fatigue, the alarm was going to go off in less than five hours, and Lisa and I had a date for tomorrow night, or I guess I mean 'tonight,' since it was already technically another day. I slid between the sheets and drifted off, thinking sweetly mingled thoughts of Jacko in my arms and Lisa on the phone. Lisa, softly handsome Lisa with the dark hair and the blue eyes and the lovely, strong, graceful body. . . . I never had told her why I wasn't at Susan's.

17

CHAPTER 4

The morning paper had Sandy's killing on the front page of the City and State section. There was nothing new in the story except time of death, between six and ten A.M., which would put it right about when the neighbors saw Dean at the house. It said the police were seeking a suspect for questioning. I wondered if they had anything like fingerprints to pin it on him, but then his prints would have been all over the place at Sandy's house, anyway, since he was over there so much. I shook my head and drank my coffee and tried to find something else to think about. It wasn't hard. Lisa's lovely face floated into my mind. Tonight, tonight.

I grinned at Ronson and scratched his curly head. "To work, to work," I told him. I got out of the lawn chair where I'd been enjoying the cool breeze of the early day and took my coffee cup back into the house, locked up, and headed for the job site.

It was another scorcher of a day. No clouds, no rain, hardly any wind at all after the morning breeze had died. The sun beat down out of a sky too bright to look at, and our shirts were soaked with sweat before we'd been working ten minutes. The new flower beds took shape, though, but I doubted that even with the permitted extra watering for new plantings (Austin was in the throes of the usual summer water rationing), the things we set out would have much of a chance of making it in this heat. "Pile that mulch on," I told my crew.

By three o'clock in the afternoon we were close enough to the end of the job that I told Cheryll and Larry to finish up while I went to mow a lawn I'd intended to get done yesterday. Lawn mowing is good work. The smells of oil and gas and fresh-cut grass, the measured pacing over the green lawn, the dependable, rhythmic racket of a Briggs and Stratton engine blotting out distracting noises — it all makes for a perfect activity to think by. Or not to think, if that's what I need. Today I thought.

I remembered going to the office of Dean Justus Caney, P.I. and talking to him about the job I wanted him to do. I'd long since quit trying to analyze why I wanted to find Claudia so much. I just missed her, even after all these years. They say your first lover is always going to be special to you, and Claudia was still special to me. I thought she would have been, even if we'd never been lovers. We were friends long before we came out, my senior year in high school. Even when we'd first met, in homemaking class when I was a junior and she was a sophomore, I'd felt completely at ease with her. There was something about her that felt to me like coming home. When I thought of that day I still felt a kind of simple, welcome peace.

Of course we'd had our hard times, but those were seldom what I thought about. They just didn't seem nearly as real, eighteen years later, as the friendship, the intimacy, the joy we had. Not that I'd been saving myself for her since then or anything. I'd had lots of lovers. But when I thought of what had been really good in my life, she was always there.

What had inspired me to go to the detective with it at last was a little money I'd come into from a paid-up life insurance policy my parents had taken out for me when I was two. It wasn't drawing much interest just sitting there, two thousand dollars that wasn't enough for a new truck or a trip to Tahiti but ought to cover expenses for a skiptrace search by a private dick. I had suppressed my distrust of men who hang around dykes and plunked my money down on Dean Caney's desk, and now I had a suspected lesbian-killer assigned to find my friend. I'd given him two hundred and fifty bucks retainer. He was probably using it for getaway money.

"I should have done it myself," I muttered under the roar of the lawnmower. But I didn't know a damn thing about finding missing persons. And why wasn't it 'missing people,' anyway? Hell, I wouldn't know how to find a missing dog.

But could skiptracing really be so hard? If a guy like Caney could do it, why couldn't I? What did he do, go to detective school or something? I'd never heard of a detective school. Except the police academy, of course. But had Caney ever been a cop? Most of the private eyes in detective novels were ex-cops. I'd read a lot of whodunits, but I couldn't remember a single one that described the mechanics of skiptracing. Most of them were just murder mysteries. I gritted my teeth. Somehow murders in books didn't seem as horrible as Sandy's real one.

Somebody that knew about it ought to write an article on skiptracing for *Lesbian Connection*, I thought. "How to Track Down Your Long-Lost Lover." I'd seen those ads in there: "So-and-so, where are you? It's been six years and I wonder how you are? Write me." I hadn't even tried that avenue. I was too impatient, or too passive, or too some other disgusting thing. I had, I decided, acted like a feminine dumb-ass. Let a man do it; it's too mysterious for little me.

"Oh, fucking hell!" I said to the lawnmower.

But getting down on myself about it wasn't going to do any good. I couldn't turn back the clock. The question was, what was I going to do about it now? Either nothing or something. If I decided 'nothing,' I'd better start thinking about something else and forget about finding Claudia. But if I decided to do something, I had to deal with the perplexing question, "What?" I didn't think Dean Caney was going to be spending much time looking up my old friend now.

But suppose he'd already gotten a lead on her? Would he have written down what he found? If he had, it would no doubt be in his office, just sitting there not doing me or anybody else any good. I loaded up the lawn mower and got in the truck. Dean Caney had a secretary. Maybe she could tell me something.

CHAPTER 5

The converted house on Powell Street where Dean Caney had his office needed the attention of a gardener bad. Somebody had put in a forlorn row of periwinkles in a little bed by the front steps, but nobody had apparently paid any attention to them after that. They were stiff now, with leaves curled crisp, the pitiful remains of a small, faded flower or two still holding on here and there. Even the few weeds that had tried to take advantage of the once-loosened soil had given up. I hate to see things like that.

Nobody was at the desk in the little waiting room. I stood listening for sounds of life, and then footsteps told me somebody was among the living here, after all. The woman I remembered from when I was here before came through the door that led to Caney's office, leaving it open behind her. I could see his big, scarred wooden desk with papers all over the top of it, just the way it had been when I'd told him my story and given him my money.

"May I help you?" she said, and then, "Oh, hello. You were here last week."

"Yes."

"Mr. Caney's not in right now. . . ." She looked tired. No doubt it wasn't easy minding the shop for a fugitive from a murder charge.

"I know," I said.

She nodded, sitting down and looking up at me.

"I was wondering—did he happen to get anything done on the case I brought him, do you happen to know?"

"I don't know. He'd be the only one who'd know about that."

"Oh." A lot of good that information was going to do me. "I wonder if I could just see the file," I said, trying to sound confident. "Just to check."

She thought a minute and then came to a decision. "I guess that'd be all right." She met my eyes with a look of resignation. "I guess nothing can hurt now, can it."

"I guess not." I wondered how she was going to get paid for keeping the office open while her boss was on the run, but it was none of my business.

She went into Dean's office again, and I followed her. The file, a plain manila folder, was lying with some others in a wire basket on the corner of the desk. She fished it out and handed it to me. I saw my name, Cass Milam, and the date I'd talked to Caney on the tab. On the outside of the folder were a few scribbled lines that looked like dates and times, one the date on the file and one for each of the next two days. If that showed how long he'd spent on the case, it looked like he'd already done about an hour's work. I flipped open the folder to see what he'd turned up.

In the folder was the single sheet of paper he'd used when he'd made notes as I talked to him, along with the contract I'd signed giving him permission to investigate and acknowledging his rates. Clipped to the sheet of notes was the snapshot I'd lent him of Claudia as she'd looked when we were new lovers. She looked very young, and very happy. In the black and white photo she stood beside me in the doorway of the garage apartment where we'd lived in Hyde Park, holding my hand, obviously, though our hands were behind us a little and out of direct sight of the photographer, who, I remembered, had been a woman who lived next door. I looked young, too, and a lot slimmer. I was smiling.

23

I didn't see anything in the notes but what I'd told Caney, except down at the bottom was scribbled what looked like, "SA, 5585 Serna Pk." I got a pencil and wrote that down. It looked like an address, so maybe it was a lead he'd turned up. That was all, though.

"I guess I'll take my picture back, anyway," I told the secretary.

"Fine," she said without interest.

But when I slipped off the paper clip that was holding the photograph to the sheet, I found there was another picture clipped on with it. I picked it up and looked at it.

Like the one of Claudia and me, this was a picture of two young women. They were both in shorts, standing on some rocks with water in the background. I could just make out blurred hills behind the water. Maybe taken up on the lakes somewhere, I guessed. These two had their arms around each other's waists, the taller one looking down possessively at the shorter one while the shorter one beamed at the camera. Lovers. I didn't know either of them, I saw in a minute. But I'd had to look twice. At first glance, I'd have sworn the shorter woman was Claudia.

Back in my truck, the two photographs lying on the seat beside me, I sat a minute to think. The strangers in the other shot were definitely not people I'd ever seen. I picked up the picture and studied it closely. The one who looked like Claudia wasn't quite built like her —wider hips and smaller breasts, different proportions of arm and leg. But the tilt of the head was the same, and the eyes and eyebrows were remarkably like hers, and so was the whole expression, though there was a heaviness about the chin and jaw that Claudia didn't have, and the nose was more prominent. A very nice-looking woman, though. Neither photo was in color, so I couldn't tell about the eyes. These looked about the same color value as Claudia's, but it would have been a wonder if they'd actually been the same. Claudia's eyes were a golden color that I'd never seen in anyone else. In fact, that was listed in the notes I'd given Caney. Her skin had had a goldish cast to it, too, and her brown-blonde hair had repeated the tone with just enough difference to set off her complexion. It wasn't from the sun, either; she was that beautiful color all over.

So who was this woman and why was she in my file? Maybe Lisa would have some ideas about it when I saw her tonight. At least it would be something to talk about besides the murder.

It was after five when I got home to Hank Street. Cheryll and Larry had already left the dooley in the drive and gone. The lawn, since I'd set the sprinklers on it with a timer this morning, looked a little less thirsty, the only mail in my box was a *Reader's Digest* sweepstakes offer with a nickel glued on it, and the cats and dog were glad to see me.

Getting home after a day at work can almost always make me smile, and tonight I had something to look forward to besides my comfortable routine. Lisa was picking me up at seven. I was whistling as I coiled up the hoses and took the sprinklers in. I sang in the shower, thinking of Lisa. I would have never guessed she'd give me a second look. I knew some of the women she'd gone with before, and I really didn't fit in with that crowd much. They were all professional types or students, and I was just an old-gay lawn mower. Lisa, though, was a factory worker, even if she didn't seem like she would be, just to meet her. I'd have to find out more about her tonight. In the meantime, why question it? I was just planning to have a good time and enjoy my good fortune. She was not only nice, she was beautiful.

She pulled up in front in her silver Toyota at twelve minutes after seven, right on schedule if you went by Dyke Standard Time, and I went out grinning and smelling enchantingly, I hoped, of Old Spice cologne. I had on my best-pressed white slacks and a pale yellow knit shirt that set off my tan-and-freckled arms. Dressed to kill, by golly.

We went to the Spanish Village and ate a lot of good food and talked about this and that. Not much about

25

Sandy and Dean at first. She asked me about my work and I told her for a long time, probably longer than she'd planned to listen, and I asked about her job and she told me briefly.

"It's really just until I find something I want in my field," she said, "but I like it. It's not demanding, and it's fun to have different hours off."

"What's your field?"

"I have my Master's in social work. I could do counseling at a couple of places in town right now, but what I'm really looking for is a little different. More job-related stuff. Career counseling. I think it's really important that people are matched up with the careers they're best suited for, so I'd like to get into that end of things."

"You ain't woofin', it's important," I said.

"You like your work."

"I do, for a fact."

"That's one of the things I like about you."

"Yeah?"

"I like to see somebody that's enthusiastic about her whole life, not just what she does after five o'clock."

"Well, that's true."

We looked into each other's eyes across the table. Her eyes were so very blue. So very, very blue.

She smiled, after a minute, and so did I. "Well." She broke the contact and scooped up the last of the salsa with the next-to-the-last tortilla chip. I breathed again. "So, do you feel like talking about the job you had Dean working on for you, or is it none of my business?"

"No, I'll tell you." I would have told her anything, I thought. It was going to be hard to get enough of looking at her in one short evening. She was just really beautiful.

So I filled her in, at least sketchily, on what I'd asked Dean to do about finding Claudia. "And the woman in the picture looked enough like her to be her twin sister," I finished.

Lisa frowned. Even her frown was beautiful. "Do you have the picture?"

26

"I have it at home," I said. "Come on back to the house and take a look."

"I'd like that."

I practically danced out of the restaurant.

CHAPTER 6

"So what do you make of it?" Lisa was sitting on my couch looking at the two photographs. I was standing. I wanted to sit down by her, but how close should I sit? I felt a little shy.

"I don't know." She held the two pictures side by side, looking at one and then the other. "They certainly do look alike."

"They do." I stepped over to look, paused a second, and then screwed up my courage and sat down beside her, close. "I thought it was Claudia myself, at first."

"It must be somebody Dean knows, I guess. Maybe he thought they were the same person."

"Maybe. Maybe he thought he actually knew Claudia and could get hold of her without going to any trouble for me."

"Could be. I don't know what else to think."

"Me, either."

We both looked at the pictures. Lisa's leg felt warm beside mine. A few seconds passed in silence. I reached for the pictures and she held onto them, too, our hands touching. I wasn't seeing the faces in the photographs any more. A few more seconds passed. I turned toward her, looking into her eyes, and she looked back solemnly. I leaned toward her, her eyes closed and her lips parted, and I took her in my arms and, very softly at first, touched her lips with mine.

The trouble with Lisa's working hours was that she had this evening off only because she was working the graveyard shift. We just had about an hour before she had to leave for work, but we made the most of it. Lord, I could have used the rest of the night. But when we finally dragged ourselves back to practical reality, she went out to her car and came back with an old pair of jeans and a work shirt.

"You brought your clothes," I said.

She smiled. "I thought I'd be prepared."

"You devil, you." I caught her and kissed her some more, and by the time she left she had hardly any time to make it across town to the plastics plant. "Are you late like this often?" I asked her as she got in her car.

"Not as often as I'd like to be."

Should I say something about maybe doing this again? Would she want to? Had she liked it? Was I just a one-night stand for her? If I asked her to come back, would it scare her off?

She saw my confusion and smiled. "Maybe we ought to start a little earlier," she said.

"Next time?"

"Yes. Next time." She kissed me through the car window and drove away. As soon as she was out of sight, I let out a warwhoop that I hoped waked the neighborhood. Lisa wanted to see me again, and I wanted the whole world to know.

I was far too energized to go to bed right away. I looked again at the two pictures. Claudia looked just as I remembered her. I wondered what she'd think of me tonight. When she and I had done these things together, we'd thought we were inventing them, almost. Now they were familiar, but still, in a way, just as new. And with Lisa, they'd been better than I remembered in a long time.

I wished I could talk to Claudia. I'd wished it for years, at times like these. She'd have liked to see me feeling happy.

And maybe I could find her. It couldn't really be so hard, if Caney and his ilk could do it. The police had a missing persons bureau, I thought. Claudia wasn't a candidate for that, but maybe they could tell me how I could start looking, anyway. And the nice thing about the cop shop is that it's always open.I looked at the number on my telephone pad and dialed the Austin Police.

"If I want to trace somebody I've lost track of for years," I asked the man who answered, "how do I start?"

The cop or whoever it was had heard this question before. He rattled off his answer as if he'd said it a hundred times. "Number one, check the DPS. Number two, check the utility companies. Number three, go through all the phone books of the towns they might live in. Number four, go to his last known address and start asking people. That's about all you can do, ma'am, unless you want to spend some money. Then you can hire a private investigator to do it for you."

"Yeah, I know. What do you mean, 'check the DPS?' I mean, who do I ask for, or—"

"Just call them in the morning and they'll tell you how to check a driving record. If he has a Texas license, they'll be able to give you the information. It's a matter of public record."

"Oh. Well, thanks." I had a hundred vague questions swimming in my head, but I couldn't think of what else specific to ask him, so I hung up.

It was a start. I jotted down the things he'd told me. Department of Public Safety. I didn't know you could get somebody else's driving record, but I guessed you could. Phone books. I'd seen a lot of out-of-town phone books at the library, but where to start looking? She could be anywhere, and this country has a lot of towns with phone books. And what if she'd changed her name? A lot of dykes do, for one reason or another. I was pretty sure Marigold couldn't have been Sandy's father's name, for instance. And old neighbors? Good luck. She'd lived in an apartment over by the university. There wouldn't be a person there who'd been there eighteen years ago, much less one who might know where a not-very-sociable young woman had gone when she left Austin.

Well, I knew where this not-so-young woman was going right now. Exhaustion had hit. As soon as I'd grabbed a quick shower, I was going to bed—this time to sleep.

"Beginning in the morning," I told Chip as he followed me into the bathroom, "I'm going to do my own detecting."

CHAPTER 7

The Texas Department of Public Safety, in the person of a woman with the reddest hair I'd ever seen, took my Request for Driving Record form and my five-dollar fee. She promised a report in the mail in a week. "It'll take them a few days to search, since you don't have the driver's license number," she told me. "You'll hear as soon as they find anything." She flicked me a small smile of dismissal. I went.

Now that I'd already taken the day off to play detective, it would be a waste not to try everything I could think of. I might as well get the least likely source out of the way first, so I headed for Claudia's old neighborhood.

She'd moved into an apartment on Rio Grande when she left me. Judy Netsy, a straight woman until she met Claudia, had been a student at the university. When she'd left her husband for Claudia, they'd gotten a place in walking distance of Judy's classes.

Summer school was in full swing. I found a parking place just two blocks from the address and hiked back there. The house was old and otherwise undistinguished. Anything that had once made its owners proud had been stripped away over the years, so that it now stood in a narrow lot with no landscaping, the front yard paved for parking and the side yards long since sold off and built over. An old and scrawny crepe myrtle straggled upward at the right-hand corner of what had been the porch, now enclosed for the apartment conversion, the sole remaining horticultural ornament of the place. I imagined someone planting it as a tiny, young bush, watering it in, watching it over the years as it grew gracefully upward to soften the outline of the square porch column. It had outlived the porch and probably the gardener, too.

Just inside the door were mailboxes, most with names written on cards or masking tape labels. No Netsy, no Fanding—Claudia's name—and no other that rang the slightest bell with me. I picked the oldest-looking card, copied the name and apartment number, and started climbing the stairs. I found the apartment, but nobody answered my knock. While I stood there debating what to try next, a movement down the hall caught my eye and I turned to see someone leaning out another door.

"He's at class. Want to leave a note for him?"

"Oh, thanks, but I guess not." I walked down the hall and the boy came out to meet me. "I was just looking for somebody who used to live here a long time ago."

"Oh, yeah? What's their name? I might know them. I've been here two years."

I laughed. "That's what I was afraid of. I'm thinking more like eighteen years."

"Wow! I'd have been about three then!"

"Time flies. I guess you don't know of any real old-timers around here? Either here or in the neighborhood?"

"Not that old."

"Well, thanks, anyway." That little exchange made me feel about the same age as the old crepe myrtle tree.

I got halfway down the block toward my truck when a thought hit me, and I turned around and hurried back to the house. "I wonder," I said to the kid when he came to his door, "if you could tell me how to get hold of your landlord?"

He snapped his fingers. "Hey, sure! Why didn't I think of that?" He scribbled down an address on a yellow sheet from a legal pad and handed it to me. "He's got a dusty office down on West Fifth. I don't know how long he's handled this place, but he looks like he's been around a while."

I thanked him, but all this reference to ancient times was beginning to sting.

The office of Shedder and Kyle, Real Estate, was behind a glass door that was, as the student had said, dusty. The building was old, the facelift it had had at one time was getting old, and the man behind the antiquated-looking, high counter was a good bit past middle age.

"May I help you?" The old man's voice was rusty but friendly.

"I hope so," I said. I told him what I was after, and he said, "Let me look."

He got down a thick account book from a row on a shelf behind him, thumbed through it, and tilted his head back to read the page through the bottom of his bifocals. "Claudia J. Fanding, apartment 1-C. Only stayed four months. Most of them stay the full semester. But we rent month-to-month over there. That way, if they don't like it, they can go. And if we don't like them, they can go, too." He smiled. "You want the address where we sent her deposit?"

"That would be great."

He wrote on the back of a rent receipt and handed it across the counter. I looked at it. The address was in San Antonio, on Serna Park Drive. Great! San Antonio was just an hour or so away on I-35.

"Hope you find her," he said.

On the way home, I stopped off and got a cheeseburger, fries, and a large cherry limeade. I spread them out on the little table by my chair in the back yard and ate, feeling pleased with myself for my morning's work. I fended off the animals by breaking off a little piece of my meat for each of the cats and Ronson, and we all munched happily.

Midway through my meal, I was thinking about what I'd found out, and it dawned on me that I'd seen Claudia's forwarding address before. I went into the house and checked, and I was right. I could have saved myself some effort. Dean Caney had already known where Claudia had gone. Her address was what he'd written on the notes in her file.

While I was staring at Caney's note, the phone rang.

"Cass? It's Lisa. Have you been listening to the news?"

"What news?"

"They found Dean's car."

"What do you mean?"

"It was parked out by the Loop 360 bridge. The keys were in it."

"What about Dean?"

"They don't know. They're dragging the lake."

"You mean they think he jumped?" I thought of that beautiful, soaring bridge and the long, long drop to the water of Lake Austin. A lovely and lonely place to die.

"When did they find it?"

"Last night."

"So I guess that means he killed her, huh?"

"And then killed himself. It looks like it. Of course, maybe he didn't jump. Maybe something just happened to his car and he walked off and left it."

"They wouldn't be dragging the lake if there was some reason for him to have left his car."

"No. I guess they wouldn't."

"Did he leave a note or anything?"

"They didn't say."

I thought a minute. Lisa was silent. Then, "Look," I said. "Could it be that he jumped off the bridge out of grief?"

"You mean over Sandy?"

"Yeah. Suppose he didn't kill her, but just found her dead. Everybody says he was crazy about her. . . ."

"Yeah, he was. But I don't think he was in love with her or anything. They were just friends. Sandy very definitely didn't sleep with men."

"Hmm. Maybe that's why he killed her?"

"Oh, god, I don't know. Maybe he isn't dead, either."

"What? You mean he could have left his car there

to fake a suicide? To get the pressure off, so the cops would stop looking for him?"

"It could be. I really didn't know him well enough to try to guess."

"I wonder who did?"

"Lucia Bolte, I imagine. She and he were pretty good friends, and she was close to Sandy."

"Have you talked to her since all this happened?"

"She's gone home for her sister's wedding. I think she ought to be back by now, though."

"I wish you'd talk to her. I'm not very convinced he's dead, without a body. And I still think that could have been him driving by my house the other day."

Lisa said, "Hmm," in a skeptical tone.

"Anyway, I've got a lead on Claudia," I said, and I told her about my day's detecting. "I thought I might run down there this afternoon and check it out," I finished.

"You're really out to find this woman, aren't you?"

"Yeah, I am. It just seems like now I've got the ball rolling, I ought to go ahead and track her down. I kind of feel like it's now or never, you know?"

"She must have meant a lot to you, Cass."

"Yeah. I'll tell you about it sometime."

"I'd like to hear about her."

"You wouldn't like to run down there with me, I guess?"

"I can't this afternoon." She didn't say why not, and I didn't inquire. I was too new in Lisa's life for her to owe me any explanations. Maybe pretty soon that would change.

"Well, wish me luck," I said. "I'll call you when I get back, or tomorrow, if it's too late."

"Good luck," she said. And she added, "And Cass, be careful." From the way she said it, I didn't think she just meant be careful on the road. I was going to try to open up a door into the past, and there had been a lot of hurt there for me. Somehow I felt like Lisa knew that.

"I will," I said.

CHAPTER 8

The highway south to San Antonio parallels the Balcones Escarpment, the dividing line between the coastal plains and the Texas hill country. On my right I had the limestone hills with their scattered quarries and on my left I had the gentler-looking grassland rolling two hundred miles or so to the Gulf. I drove along with the wind like a blast furnace through the truck windows, admiring the land and wishing I owned a nice chunk of it. I thought about our old dreams, Claudia's and mine, of owning a place where we could have horses. There'd be a field of wildflowers, a row of crepe myrtles along the drive, white board fences. . . .

I really hadn't thought about these things in years, but this summer they seemed always to be coming to the surface like springs along a fault zone, making me restless and nostalgic. It was probably just that I was getting close to forty, I told myself. Midlife crisis or something. My life was sure turning out different from what I'd expected when Claudia and I were dreaming those old dreams.

I'd never thought I'd end up in the landscape and mowing business, but it was what I'd drifted into after she'd gone with Judy Netsy. Somehow over the years I'd settled down and made a go of it. I'd even commuted the thirty miles to San Marcos a couple of semesters to take some horticulture courses, and I'd gotten a couple more from Penn State by correspondence. Austin Community College had given me the instruction I'd needed in small engine repair, another aspect of the business I'd enjoyed. All in all, I was looking like being set in this line of work for life.

But Claudia had never been far from my mind. Nobody'd ever come along to replace her, and now I wanted to tie up this old, loose end and get on with my life. It seemed like it was time I ought to quit remembering and get on with living.

I felt good about what I was doing, finally doing something to lay the ghost of my old love to rest. As I drove I let myself think of life with Claudia the way I hadn't allowed myself to in years. I'd come to think of those days as wonderful, and in a lot of ways they were. Love was new and sex was new and every experience life had to offer was coming to us for the first time. We might as well have been the first lesbians ever; we thought we were the greatest thing that ever happened.

Or was that just what I thought? I remembered now that Claudia had always had a very practical streak running through her youthful romanticism. There had been a lot of little things she'd done and said that should have told me she was looking out for number one, even at the expense of our relationship. She wanted a lot out of life, and one of the things she wanted was to move in more sophisticated circles than either of us ever had. She hung out with college kids, drama majors, and arty types mostly. She read magazines like The New Yorker, she made her own clothes from Vogue patterns, and she cooked with recipes out of Gourmet. If she had pocket money, she'd spend it on something fancy at an antique store. I remembered a chipped but elegant crystal Scotch decanter she'd brought home once. She'd spent our grocery money on that.

But she also swore she loved me, and she did little nice things for me like leaving me funny, handmade cards to find when I got up in the morning before her. And she was the most sensuous, skillful, responsive lover I ever had, bar none, and that includes some sexy women.

Judy Netsy had been an art major at U.T. I hadn't considered her a threat to me, because she was straight and married. To me, she was just one of the people Claudia liked to run around with. I couldn't believe it when I'd realized what was going on, and by then it was too late. She'd been more what Claudia wanted than I was, I guess. But I couldn't have been any different if I'd wanted to, could I? Well, I'd find Claudia now and see that she was okay, and then I'd go on with my life in Austin, with my friends and my work, and . . . with Lisa? Too early to tell. I had to get this out of the way first.

I-35 unrolled beneath my wheels, and the sun glared down and shimmered heat waves over the pavement, while I thought and dreamed of my young, true love from long ago. The miles moved easily by, the truck wheels sang on the road, and Dean Caney passed me in a red Jeep Cherokee. Either him or his dead-ringer double.

CHAPTER 9

I found out the meaning of the phrase, 'paralyzed with shock.' I was simply frozen for a second or two, hands gripping the wheel, eyes straight ahead, seeing nothing but the back of that red Cherokee pulling away in the inside lane, the driver never once, as far as I could tell, glancing into his rearview mirror. And, now that I could breathe again and take my foot off the accelerator to let him get a lot of distance on me as quickly as possible, I thought he hadn't even looked over as he'd passed me. I'd glanced at him and seen only his profile, his eyes fixed on the road ahead.

I would have thought the jolt I felt when I recognized him would have been strong enough to jump between us like a lightning bolt and jerk his head around. But it hadn't, and now his Jeep was vanishing over a rise in the distance, still going the same speed.

But had he recognized me as he came up behind me? I slowed down, pulled onto the shoulder, and stopped. The last I'd heard, the police were dragging the lake. If the man had been dead, the question of his guilt in Sandy's murder would still be open. But if that was really Caney who passed me, and I'd stake my life it was, then he wasn't in the lake at all, and the conclusion that led to was obvious. Dean Caney alive after a faked suicide just about had to be a killer.

What if he had recognized me as he came up behind me, and what if he'd thought I'd recognize him? He'd killed one woman; would he stop at killing another one to get away? What if he was waiting for me over the next hill?

I sat there with the engine idling and listened to the quiet breeze hissing over the dry grass by the road, a soft sound that, under normal circumstances, would have seemed peaceful. Now it reminded me of the buzzing of a coiled rattlesnake. I kept my eyes glued on the top of the hill and caught my breath as a red car top rose into view in the northbound lane. It was followed immediately by the rest of a sedan of some kind, and I sighed and considered what to do.

What if Dean were waiting up there? What could he do? Block the road? Not with just one vehicle, he couldn't. Two south-bound lanes, paved shoulders, a grassy median—I could get by him. Could he shoot me? I supposed he owned a gun, though I'd never heard it mentioned. And so what if he hadn't owned one before? He also hadn't owned a red Jeep Cherokee before. In fact, as far as I knew, he hadn't killed anybody before, either.

So, if he had a gun and was waiting to shoot me, what were his chances? Pretty good, I thought, if he was any kind of a shot. Unless. . . . Could my truck outrun his Jeep? I only had a six-cylinder engine, but the truck was light and I'd be going flat-out when I crested the hill. If he was stopped there waiting for me, he couldn't hope to catch me from a standing start before I could get somewhere I could attract attention and get help. And he probably wouldn't risk shooting at me if another car —I stepped on the accelerator, popped the clutch, and jumped the truck out onto the road, revving up hard through the gears. The eighteen-wheeler I'd spotted in my mirror was roaring right beside me as I came over the rise, so I could only see the outside shoulder of the road and not the median, but on my side of the highway, at least, there was not a sign of any red Jeep. I stayed with the semi as I watched the mirror, and soon I could see that the median side of the pavement was empty, too. I slowed down, waved at the trucker as he pulled away, and grinned with relief. No telling what the truck driver thought I was up to, but I bet I gave him an interesting diversion for a minute there.

Now. Should I stop in New Braunfels, the town which the road signs told me was coming right up, or should I turn around at the next overpass and scuttle back to Austin with my tail between my legs? Or should I just go on to San Antonio like nothing had happened? It seemed to me that Dean must not have even seen me to recognize me, so he was probably preoccupied with something besides effecting my immediate demise. The fact that he hadn't noticed me probably meant he hadn't been looking for me, or if he had noticed me, he was probably banking on my not noticing him. He probably just wanted to get as far from Austin as fast as he could.

Now that I thought about it, San Antonio, a much bigger city than Austin, would be a good place for him to hide out. Chances of my running into him down there were slim. I decided to go on.

It might do to get a little more distance between us, though. I pulled off an exit ramp and ran along the service road until I came to a gas station. And there was another thing I ought to do. I got out and dropped some money in the pay phone and called the Austin Police.

I told them where I was and what I'd seen, and the woman I talked to asked me if I'd hold a minute. I said I would, the line clicked, and a familiar voice said, "Alcorn."

I identified myself and repeated what I'd just told the woman on the switchboard. I couldn't tell if it excited Sgt. Alcorn or not.

"Did you get a license number on this vehicle?"

"No." I'd already been kicking myself about that, but I'd been too shocked to notice any license number and I didn't feel like I needed to apologize for it. I'm not a cop, after all.

"Okay. Now, did this man, did he identify you or look at you, or look like he knew who you were?"

I described the whole incident in detail then, putting in my reactions and telling what I'd done and why. At the end of my story, Alcorn grunted in a tone that I took to mean grudging approval.

"Okay, Cassandra, we'll take it from here. No need for you to be playing cops and robbers, now."

"Playing, hell!"

"Thank you for calling." He hung up. The phone rang immediately and I followed the operator's instructions and deposited another fifty cents. My contribution to law and order for the day.

CHAPTER 10

I'm a cool and collected customer, I thought as I strolled from the pay phone to the office of the gas station. Boy, I handled that just right with Caney, and with Sgt. Alcorn, too. I can keep my head in a crisis, okay.

I picked a root beer out of the cooler at the back of the station office and set in on the counter. The attendant rang it up and told me, "Fifty-three cents." I pulled the change out of my pocket, turning my pocket inside out in the process, dropped what seemed like about five-hundred coins on the floor, started picking up the coins and dropped my keys. I got a couple of quarters and a nickel on the counter at last and recovered most of my property from the floor. I snatched up the root beer, didn't quite drop it, and told the attendant, "Keep the change."

Back in the truck I took a deep breath and held it, leaned my head back, and closed my eyes. When I let the breath go, I felt better. Not so shaky. Not so clumsy, either, I hoped. God, how could I think I was so cool? I drank the root beer slowly and watched the light traffic go by. Do cops get used to this sort of thing? Just the passing glimpse of a bad guy had completely thrown me. Big, brave dyke.

I finished the root beer and walked over and tossed the empty in a trash can. I thought of the state's anti-litter slogan, "Don't Mess with Texas." Maybe I needed a sign on my truck, "Don't Mess with Milam." Scare off any murderers I might meet on the road. Scare off any cus-

44

tomers for my business, too. If I wasn't losing them already by not being home during the days to answer the phone. I thought, not for the first time, that I ought to invest in an answering machine. Then I could get calls during the day and not just after work and in the mornings. It might pay for itself. On the other hand, I hate the damn things when I'm trying to call somebody and get their cutesy message and a beep. I can never talk to one and sound natural. I usually hang up. But some people must not mind them, or so many people wouldn't have them. And even if somebody didn't want to talk to the thing, it would at least be better than no answer at all. At least they'd know I was still in business.

These thoughts kept my mind occupied long enough for me to get into the outskirts of San Antonio. I watched the speedometer closely as I went through the famous speed trap at Selma, but the cop was working the other side of the road this afternoon. Then it was time to start watching for my exit.

San Antonio had grown a lot since I'd been down here last. Too, I'd always been here at night before, to go to the bars. It looked different in the daytime. Except for the diabolical maze of its streets, this had always seemed like a comfortable and friendly town. Lots more Spanish spoken here than in Austin, though. If I ever lived here, I'd want to learn it.

I found my exit and took it, checking by glancing at the map folded open on the seat, and I didn't even make one wrong turn getting to Serna Park Drive. It was in a middle-class neighborhood, Anglo, with houses that probably cost around fifteen-thousand dollars twenty years ago. Good-sized yards, most of them kept up pretty well, and everything looking lusher and more tropical than Austin somehow, even though just about seventy miles separated the two towns. I saw shrubs I didn't know, and the ones I did know were obviously getting a lot more favorable growing conditions than the ones in Austin, it looked like. There must be a difference in rainfall and maybe in winter temperature or something. Plants

45

will show you differences people will never notice. Anyway, they sure must not have water rationing.

I drove slowly along the street and studied the landscaping and thought of Claudia in this setting. It was certainly a step up from our old garage apartment in Hyde Park. Also from her little nest with Netsy in the old house on Rio Grande. Up was the direction she wanted to go, all right, but I would have pictured her gravitating to someplace more sophisticated or artsy than this. The King William district, maybe. I'd been to a party over there one time, and it seemed like a much more likely place for Claudia than this. Very old, very fancy houses from the early days of San Antonio, already getting expensive even back when I was there, because the area was becoming fashionable again, kind of the way Hyde Park had in Austin. There'd still been a few houses with apartments in them then, but really rich people were buying and restoring the old places, and the prices were, of course, going up. It would have suited Claudia perfectly. This area, on the other hand, looked like something a straight family would have liked. Proper for Judy Netsy and her husband.

Claudia and Judy had met in an art gallery. Claudia had struck up a conversation with her about the paintings, and when she came home that day, I remember she told me about it. It was about this time of year, July or August, and for some reason I remember the clothes she was wearing then, blue pants and a wide-shouldered, loose-fitting blouse of some soft material, cut in a broad vee neck. It was a pale yellow print with tiny flowers on it like the print on old-fashioned flour sacks. Thinking about it made me remember, with a sharpness that I felt from my chest clear down to my belly, how it felt to take Claudia by the shoulders and feel her flesh through that soft material, run my hands lightly down and over her breasts, feel her breathing change . . . and the way she'd turn her face up to me with her eyes closed and her lips parted and smiling at the same time. . . . Oh god, oh god, we were so . . . so *good* at it. Jesus, I've never known

46

anybody like her, so sensuous and so warm and so passionate. . . .

This wasn't good for me. It wasn't even good for my driving. I nearly ran a stop sign, and there was a car coming, too. I shook my head angrily. She was wonderful, I was wonderful with her, we were the greatest lovers in the world — and she left me for this straight woman from this pricky art gallery that hung all abstracts that never sold because they looked like shit. The place closed after one summer, and it deserved to. And that at least meant I didn't have to look at it every time I passed that way and remember my wonderful lover like I was doing now — endangering everybody on the streets of San Antonio.

I found the address and parked at the curb. The house was a little run down but comfortable looking. Green asbestos shingle siding, darker green trim, car port instead of a garage. There was a picture window looking out onto the front porch; the curtains were closed. I got out of the truck, walked to the front door on legs turned suddenly to jelly, and rang the doorbell.

Nothing happened.

I waited a minute and rang again. I could hear the faint chime from inside, but nothing else. The lack of response made me braver; I opened the screen and knocked on the wooden door. As I'd suspected, nobody was home.

Feeling both frustrated and relieved, I went back and sat in the truck to decide what to do. There was a sweet breeze blowing through the truck windows. It was hot, but the heat seemed to lack that baking quality I'd been noticing at home lately. It didn't feel horribly humid, but there was a softness about the air that I liked. I remembered the nights feeling this way when I used to come down here to the bars in the summertime, a sort of subtropical feeling that relaxed me, and I was relaxing now. After all, I was off the hook. I'd tried the only lead I had and come up empty. If Claudia had opened the door, I don't know what I'd have done. Now I could just go home and wait to see what the DPS turned up for me.

But conscience got the better of me. I knew very well that I still could ask the neighbors here and maybe get another lead. This looked like a lot more stable area than the old university neighborhood, and there was a chance somebody here might really know something from that long ago. I sighed. Okay, I'd do it.

The houses on either side of the one I was interested in showed no signs of life, but the one right across the street had a car in the drive. I climbed out of the truck, adjusted my collar and tugged on my shirttail to unstick the shirt from my sweaty back, and walked over there.

CHAPTER 11

A woman, middle-aged, wearing loose jeans and a faded blue blouse, examined me through the screen. "Yes?" she said. There was no cordiality in her tone.

"Hello," I said, and gave her my best smile. "I'm trying to find an old friend who used to live across the street, there." I gestured toward the green-shingled house."

"Who was it?"

"Her name was Claudia Fanding, and I think she was sharing the house with another woman named Judy Netsy. It would have been seventeen or eighteen years ago when they came here."

"I figured that's who you wanted." She looked me up and down with distaste. "I don't know where they are."

Well, nobody ever said I don't look like a dyke. "But you know who I'm talking about?" I said.

"Oh, yes. Judy and Claudia. Quite a pair." She curled her lip. "No, I certainly wouldn't know where they are."

She made a move to close the door, and I said, "Wait!" She paused, looking displeased, and I said in a pleading tone, "Please, ma'am. If you can just tell me when they left, or anything that might help me find them." I cast about hurriedly for some reason to encourage her to forget her hostility and help me. "Her mother asked me to find her. Claudia's mother. She's dying of cancer and she really wants to make up with Claudia before she dies." Sometimes I can lie so fluently, I amaze myself. "She doesn't have much time left, the doctors say."

I watched the expression on her face and didn't see it soften much. She pursed her lips and stared over my right shoulder for a minute while I stood on one foot, then the other, and tried to look sincere and desperate. Finally she said, "Claudia's mother?"

"Yes, ma'am." I felt excited and pleased with myself for thinking of a story so fast and having the nerve to tell it. Cass Milam, detective. I kept a serious face.

"I don't know why she'd want her back," the woman said, "the way they used to carry on. It was a circus over there. Yelling and hollering at all hours of the night. It was enough to wake the dead. My husband used to have to go over there and bang on the door to get them to shut up. And they weren't a bit nice to him, not a bit. Not civil. Why, I wouldn't repeat what that Judy said to him one time. 'Mind your own so-and-so business' — only she didn't say 'so-and-so,' she used the word. I never heard a girl use that word. Just a common tramp. I told Jack we ought to call the police on them, but he wouldn't do it. I would have, but they quieted down. I said to Jack, 'the very next time they start this carrying on and interrupting decent people's sleep, I'm calling the police and I hope they carry them both off to jail where people like that belong.' And if you're one of those, and you look like one to me, I'm sorry, but that's what I believe. The good Lord didn't put us here to live like that, and that's what I told that Judy, I said, 'Male and female created He them,' and that's all I know. If it's in the Bible and it's against the law, that's good enough for me. I pity your kind, but you ought to go off and live with your own kind and leave decent people alone. This is a nice neighborhood."

I forced my clenched teeth apart. This was the first person I'd found who knew anything about Claudia and Judy, and I wanted what she knew.

50

"But when did they move out?" I said. "Do you remember?" I added, "Her mother really wants to see her." I made my tone as neutral as I could, considering the adrenaline that was coursing through my body.

"Oh, I remember, all right! First that Judy came home with a man and they'd stay there all afternoon together. That went on for a couple of weeks, and then your friend Claudia came home and caught them at it, and there was more screaming and hollering than you'd believe, and the man came out and got in his car and left here screeching his tires. After that things quieted down for a few days, and the next thing you know, the house is empty and both of them are gone, and I heard the place was a real mess. Food in the refrigerator and trash all over the place — just what you'd expect."

"So you saw the inside of the house after they left?"

She looked disgusted. "No, I didn't, but Mrs. Polk that lives right over there next to it did, when the real estate lady came to see about it. I was in the hospital at the time having my gall bladder out, so I wasn't here when they went through there. But I heard about it all, I can tell you. And you people wonder why normal, decent people don't want you in the neighborhood. I don't see how you-all can live like that. Well, maybe you don't," she amended, seeing my purple face, "but they sure did."

"Does Mrs. Polk still live there?" I was either going to deck this woman or die of apoplexy pretty quick, here.

"Oh, she lives there, all right. We're not transients like your friends were. We own our homes."

"Thank you," I said. I spun around and half ran down her walk to the street. I figured she'd be on the telephone to Mrs. Polk before I could get over there. Damn, I thought, which house did she mean when she said it was the one next door? I remembered her eyes shifting over my left shoulder when she said it, so that must be the one. I hadn't heard her door close behind me, so I hoped she

51

was still standing there watching me and not running to the phone. I slowed down, drew deep breaths to steady myself, and walked up the sidewalk of a salmon-colored house with white trim. I rang the doorbell, and only then did I hear the solid thunk of the door across the street being closed.

CHAPTER 12

I stood on the little, square front porch of Mrs. Polk's house and waited. The door was closed, but the windows on either side of it were open and inside I could see curtains blowing in the breeze, probably from an attic fan. I immediately felt a kinship with the occupants. The trouble with air-conditioning is that you don't get any fresh air or any breeze. How can you appreciate a cold beer or a hot bath or any of the other delicious contrasts life has to offer if you're hermetically sealed off from the weather all the time? The cordiality I might have felt for these particular kindred spirits was considerably dampened, though, by the little interview I'd just had across the street. If this Mrs. Polk was that woman's buddy, I could expect more of the same, and I hoped I could go home this evening instead of becoming the guest of the Bexar County jail. My potential for committing assault with intent to do grievous bodily harm was running just a little high.

No response to the doorbell. I'd heard it ring, ding-donging loudly through the open windows, but I heard no approaching footsteps. I was about to ring again, when the door opened suddenly, making me jump. At first I didn't see anybody there, but then I lowered my focus and looked into the face of a thin, old man in a wheel-chair. He looked up at me from dark brown eyes whose liveliness contrasted shockingly with his colorless skin and skeletal features. He smiled, showing a neat row of piano-key dentures.

"Hello, sir," I said. "I was looking for Mrs. Polk."

"You were, were you?"

"Yes, sir. Does she live here?"

"Oh, I reckon she does."

"Is she home now? I'd like to speak to her if she is."

The old man smiled wider, enjoying the game. "Well, she just might be. What'd you want to see her about?"

"Well, I was trying to locate a friend of mine who used to live next door here," I jerked my head in the direction of the house I meant, "and the lady across the street seemed to think Mrs. Polk might know something about her. Could I talk to her?" I was beginning to wonder if Mrs. Polk was in as bad a shape as Mr. Polk, if that's who this was. Would she be bedridden? Would she be too queer-hating to talk to me without having a stroke or something? Was she even home at all?

The old man spun his wheelchair and rolled a few feet down the hall away from the door. "Earlene! Earlene! Somebody wants to talk to you! Front door!" His voice was surprisingly loud and had a high-pitched, carrying quality. He swiveled back to face me looking pleased. "I can still holler, young lady." He turned his chair again and called, "Earlene! Don't keep this gal waiting, here!"

Footsteps answered him, and a woman appeared from a doorway behind him. She had neatly curled hair with a hair net over it, silver-grey with traces of that lavender color that beauty shops like to put on grey hair, and she was wiping her hands on a white cotton apron that showed streaks of what looked like fresh dirt. She said, "Darrell, hush! They can hear you in the next block!" and to me, "Hello, there! I hope you weren't waiting too long." She darted a look at Darrell, grinning in his wheel chair. "I was out in the garden on my knees, and I don't get up as fast as I did when I was your age."

"Oh, no ma'am." I smiled at the old man. "That's all right."

She stood smiling expectantly, so I plunged in. "I was looking for a friend, an old friend who used to live in the house next door. I need to get in touch with her, and that's the last address I could find for her. Claudia Fanding. It was about seventeen years ago that she lived there."

"She says a lady across the street sent her," the old man put in. "Ain't no lady lives across the street, that I know of."

"Darrell! You hush, now." She shook her head at me, but her smile was for the old man. "Don't you pay any attention to my husband. He's too mischievous for his own good." She sidestepped around the wheelchair and unlatched the screen door. "Come on in, honey. I need to get my hands washed. You come on back to the kitchen."

I pulled open the screen and went in, latching it behind me, and followed Darrell's wheelchair down the front hall and through the door into the kitchen. Through a pair of sliding glass doors, I could see a back yard that looked almost like pictures I'd seen of English cottage gardens, an amazing variety of flowers, vegetables, foliage plants, dwarf fruit trees, and even some herbs I recognized, like borage and sage. Borage for Courage, the herb lore went. And, 'Where sage grows, a woman rules.' I wasn't a bit sure who ruled here, but the courage in this household was evident.

The beds and borders were immaculate, not a dead leaf, an overblown flower, or a sign of a weed anywhere. The paths between the planted areas were wide enough for the wheelchair and surfaced in a fine, hard-packed, red crushed stone like the Hike and Bike trails in Austin. A big cedar elm shaded one corner of the yard and a concrete patio was there with lawn chairs and a wrought iron table. I walked directly to the door and stood staring at the scene. I'd never seen anything like it except maybe in the pages of *Horticulture*.

"Oh, she does like to work in that garden." The old man's voice behind me startled me; I'd been caught up in the view. "Go on. Go on out there. Get a good look. She don't mind. She'll drag you out there herself, when she comes back." I hesitated, then slid the screen open and stepped onto the patio. "Earlene! Outside!" The man rolled his chair over a little ramp at the door sill and followed me out. He wheeled to the edge of the concrete and smiled up at me. "Come on! Let's go look at it. You like flowers, or vegetables?"

"Both. I like them together." I paced slowly along the path behind his chair, listening to the tiny crunching the wheels made as they rolled over the gravel. The breeze rustled the leaves of the little fruit trees and wafted the scent of basil over the yard. This was a little paradise of a garden. Somebody ought to do an article about it for a magazine. What an incredible amount, not just of knowledge and time, but of sheer, muscle-aching work had gone into this. The scrape of the sliding door made me turn, and Mrs. Polk was standing on the patio looking at me and beaming.

"It's my pastime," she said. "Do you like gardening?"

"Pastime!" I beamed back at her. "You're an expert. Did you do all this yourself?"

"Oh, no, honey. I got a boy to do all the heavy work for me. I'm not King Kong!"

"But you planned it all?"

"Oh, yes." She laughed. "I'm still planning it. It keeps changing all the time."

"She never could make up her mind," the old man said. "First she wants it over here, then she wants it over there, then she wants it back again. That's a woman's privilege, you know. To change her mind. Place never looks the same from one week to the other."

"He's just complaining because he has to carry everything back and forth for me. I just put the plants in his lap and he carries them around where I need them. Just because he's in that chair doesn't mean I don't put him to work."

"Well, you both do a beautiful job. If you lived in Austin, I'd hire you both. I do landscaping for a living."

"You do? I thought that was a man's job. But these days the girls are just doing anything and everything, and I think it's fine."

"Time the women took on a little of the work," said her husband.

We settled around the table on the patio and Mrs. Polk poured us iced tea from an insulated jug. "So you're a friend of Claudia's?" she said. "That poor girl, I hadn't thought about her in years."

"Yes. We were friends years ago."

"Such a sweet girl. That was just after Darrell had his accident that they moved in over there." She looked toward the house next door. "We were in a state, trying to get adjusted to everything, and that girl was just as friendly as could be. She used to stay with Darrell when I had to go to the store or anything like that—that was before he learned how to get around by himself much."

"Don't need help, now." The old man smiled. "Do everything myself. Just like I always did. Can't keep me down, Earlene, can you? Wish you could, sometimes, don't you?" He winked broadly at me. "Sometimes you wish you could."

"Be quiet, Darrell," his wife said. "This girl wants to know about Claudia." She turned back to me. "Oh, Claudia was just such a wonderful neighbor. I don't know what we'd have done without her. Just as considerate and nice. . . ."

"I heard she and Judy didn't get along too well."

Mrs. Polk sighed. "No, honey, they didn't see eye to eye. I don't know what the trouble was; I didn't think it was any of my business. I got the idea there was a man involved. But it worked out all right in the end. They moved away together, she and Judy did. We used to get a Christmas card from them for a couple of years, but then they stopped sending them."

"You mean you had their forwarding address?"

"Oh, of course we did, honey. They asked me to turn in the keys to the real estate lady for them and call somebody to clean the house for them after they were out of it. They moved over closer to St. Mary's. That's where Claudia was going to school, you know."

"No, I didn't know. Do you happen to know what she was studying?"

"She was learning to be a teacher. The kind they have for slow children in the schools. What did she call it?"

"Special Education?"

"Yes, that's it. I hope she got to do that. I know she'd just be so good at it. She was the sweetest girl; I know those poor kids would just love her."

"I don't suppose you'd still have her address?"

"Why, I think I must." She got up. "I'll check. You and Mr. Polk have some more tea."

I poured tea for both of us and turned in my chair so I could look out over the jewel of a garden. "Your garden is so beautiful," I said, "I wish I had a picture of it. Not a photograph, I mean a painting. I'd love to hang it in my living room."

"Couldn't nobody paint it."

"Why not?"

"Never stays the same long enough. If she reads about a new plant in one of them garden books, in it goes. Something new all the time."

The screen door slid back in its track and Mrs. Polk came out looking pleased and carrying a slip of paper in her hand. "Here it is," she said.

I took the slip and read the neatly printed address. "Thank you," I said. "I'd better get going, but it sure has been nice meeting you both, and your garden is lovely."

Mrs. Polk beamed. "You come back and see us and let us know if you find Claudia. And when you find her, tell her we're still thinking about her."

"I will. I'd love to see your garden again."

"Won't be the same," Mr. Polk said. "Never is, one week to the next." He winked at me.

CHAPTER 13

 B ack in the truck, I looked at the address Mrs. Polk had given me and at the San Antonio map. The street was clear over on the southwest side of town, and where I was was northeast. I looked at my watch: nearly four-thirty. I could go over there and look for the address which I was pretty certain wasn't where I'd find Claudia and Judy by now, or I could call it a day and go on back to Austin.

When I thought of home, exhaustion hit me like a bulldozer. Aftershock from all that adrenaline I'd released while I was listening to that horrible dyke-hater, I guessed. Anyway, I was flat-out whipped.

In a way, it seemed stupid to go home without check-ing every possible lead down here, but on the other hand, even if I could drag myself across an unfamiliar city in the rush hour and confront some more possibly hostile people, I had no guarantee it would get me anywhere. I had two leads, the outdated address from Mrs. Polk and the information that Claudia had been studying Special Ed at St. Mary's University. If one didn't pan out, maybe the other would. If those didn't work, I thought there surely must be some way to find a Texas teacher through the Texas Education Agency, and that was back home in Austin. I was broiling in my own sweat sitting here in the truck, anyway. I'd parked it in the shade, but the shade had moved. I wanted to go home.

When I stopped to get a Coke at a gas station on my way out, I did do one other thing, one I should have thought of even before I came down here. I looked in the San Antonio phone book. There was not one Fanding or Netsy listed. I tried information, too. Nothing. On the whole, that was not good news, but it made me feel a little better for the moment. At least I wasn't giving up for the day while Claudia was just waiting somewhere in town to be found, unless she had an unlisted number.

The drive back to Austin was uneventful. No speed cops, car wrecks, passing murderers, or anything like that to make it interesting. I kind of stepped on it and got home by six. Not bad time, considering getting out of San Antonio and into Austin in the rush hour. The dooley was in the driveway, Ronson was in the back yard, the cats were in the house, and a cold beer was out of the refrigerator and on its way down my throat just as soon as I got inside. And the phone started ringing as I was walking into the bathroom and unbuttoning my pants. I cursed and grabbed up the receiver on the second ring.

"Cass? It's Lisa."

"Good, because if it had been a business call, my bladder wouldn't have stood it. Can I call you back in a minute? I just got in."

She said, "Sure, babe," and I hung up and headed for the bathroom. 'Babe?' I thought. Well, well. I was fairly sure she'd picked that up from me. It was a little old-fashioned for a modern lesbian-feminist like Lisa, but I loved the way it sounded coming from her. Kind of affectionate, kind of intimate. I didn't know, maybe this was going to become more than just a casual thing with her. I got a warm sensation when I heard her voice. Of course, that could just be the relief of hearing a dyke again after an afternoon that seemed like about a year in San Antonio wandering among heterosexuals. As soon as I stripped off my sweaty clothes and threw them in the hamper, I called her back.

"Everything come out all right?"

I groaned. "Can't you do better than that? Here I thought you were a classy lady."

"Lady be damned. Did you find Claudia?"

"Nope. I got a couple of leads, though. It was interesting, to say the least. What are you doing tonight?" Christ! Why was I asking her that? Not only was I dead beat, but I had a ten-acre tractor mowing job to do in the morning.

"Coming over for fajitas? If I bring the fajitas?"

"Get a six-pack, too."

"I'm on my way."

I showered and put on my oldest, softest cut-offs and a ragged chambray shirt that was faded almost white from many washings, fed the animals, and went out in the back yard with a beer and a tennis ball. Ronson spied the ball at once and began bounding up in great leaps as high as my head, making little delighted noises. I threw the ball for him until I was tired. Then I sat down in my chair and threw it some more. I could have gone on until my arm dropped off and he wouldn't have been ready to quit. Retrieving is his business, his pleasure, and his main thought in life. He thinks about it the way I think about loving women—the best thing a body can do, and the most natural thing in the world. I've always said if I chased off a burglar, Ronson would run catch him and drag him back.

Lisa and the fajitas arrived, and I'd be hard put to say which I was happier to see. That cheeseburger at noon was a long way back down the road. She made herself some iced tea to go with her fajitas and I stuck to beer. She'd bought Shiner, my favorite, and you can't get it just anywhere. She'd noticed it was my brand the other night, I guessed. Interesting, and nice.

We gave our full attention to eating for a while, and then after we started slowing down, she asked me questions about San Antonio. I told her in great detail while she commented just often enough to keep me talking. Whether it was real interest or social worker training I didn't know, but it sure made her easy to talk to.

61

When I'd finished, Lisa sat thinking over my story for a minute and then said, "So you're sure it was Dean you saw on the road?"

"I'm as sure as I can be, unless he has a twin brother."

"Hm. Well, I did find out something that might shed some light on things, if I knew what to make of it."

"What's that?"

"I talked to Lucia. She got back last night from her sister's wedding. She said Dean was really carrying the torch, all right, but not entirely for Sandy. It seems he had an old girlfriend years ago who turned out to be gay. He wanted to marry her, even after she decided to come out, but she broke it off with him. He never got over it, it seems. That was apparently why he started hanging around dykes. It seems odd that he'd do that; you'd think he'd never want anything to do with us after that. But Lucia said he claimed that it had showed him that lesbians were really the kind of women he liked to be around, even if it meant no romantic involvement."

"Kind of weird, isn't that?"

"Yeah. It seems like it to me. Anyway, she said he was just a nice, unobtrusive guy most of the time, but once in a while he'd get drunk and maudlin, and then all he could talk about was how much he loved that woman and how she'd run off with some dyke."

"Oh, yeah?"

"Yes. And the weirdest thing was that a couple of weeks ago Sandy told Lucia that Dean had come over to her house drunk and called her 'Marilyn.' That was the old girlfriend's name."

"But he was drunk, right?"

"Yeah, I guess. Lucia said Sandy didn't think he was drunk enough to make that kind of mistake, though. It kind of worried her."

"It'd worry me."

We sat for a few minutes, me drinking my beer and Lisa her tea. Caney was beginning to sound pretty scary to me. A guy with a romantic obsession about lesbians wasn't too healthy, I thought.

"So what are you going to do," she said when I was finished. "Go back tomorrow?"

I told her about the mowing job I had lined up. "If I get started on it about daylight, I can get home by dark, barring the unforeseen."

"So you want to get a good night's sleep then, right?"

"Right. I'd better. I feel like a dish rag. Detecting isn't a piece of cake."

"Mowing's easier?"

"By a long shot."

She got up and gathered up the supper things. I followed her into the house, and we washed our plates and silverware standing next to each other at the sink, her washing and me drying. I was putting up the last plate, when Lisa moved behind me and slipped her arms under mine. She brought her hands up and stroked the sides of my neck, holding me pinned against her. Her hands were wet and slippery with soapy water, and she slid the tips of her fingers along the tendons of my neck in a slow, sensuous motion that sent chills to my toes. I leaned back against her and closed my eyes while her hands released my shoulders and slipped under my shirt, skin against skin, and I forgot about mowing pastures or detecting or anything else except what this lovely woman was making me feel. We didn't get too much sleep that night, but I sure felt relaxed in the morning.

I didn't run into any problems with the tractor or the field I was mowing. There was no brush I couldn't cut, there were no old pieces of junk or strands of barbwire to foul up my mower, and enough clouds raced by overhead all day to keep me from burning to a crisp. The temperature had dropped a little since the week before and was only around ninety-five by four o'clock. It made a big difference. I sang until I was practically hoarse, all the fine old songs I could think of, "The Rivers of Texas," "Rambler-Gambler," "Bound to Follow the Longhorn Cow," and all my fifties rock-and-roll favorites. I wasn't really in love with Lisa, I told myself, but I had to admit I was sure taking an interest.

By the time I was through and loading up my outfit on the trailer behind the dooley, I was about fagged out, but I was still cheerful as a meadowlark. I hadn't once thought of Sandy's murdered body all day, and the incidents with Dean Caney didn't seem any more real than a movie. I'd done a lot of detecting yesterday, met some nice people and one of the other kind, seen the prettiest garden I'd ever seen, and come home to the arms of one of the handsomest women in town. Today I'd mowed ten acres in eight hours and a little more, sung myself hoarse, grinned until my face was sore, and made two hundred and twenty-five dollars. The owner of the place had already stopped by an hour before and given me a check. You couldn't beat it.

Driving home, I went by Jacko's place, taking up a whole row of spaces in her apartment complex parking lot with my rig, and knocked on her door for a while. Either she wasn't home or she was busy, because she didn't come to the door. I climbed in the dooley and went on home.

Saturday night and no plans at all, except to catch up on my domestic chores and read a good book. I bundled up my dirty clothes and picked up the morning paper that I hadn't had a chance to read yet and put that stuff, a box of Cheer, and a cold beer in the back of the stepside truck. Going to the laundromat is not my favorite job, but there's no place in my house where I could fit in a washing machine if I had one. I got a parking space right in front of the door, took my things in, and got them in the machines. I changed a couple of dollars in the change machine, started my stuff washing, and relinquished my good parking place while I drove over to the Whataburger and got a cheeseburger, an order of fries, and an order of their wonderful onion rings. Back at the laundromat, I parked up where the light from the sign over the entrance was enough to read by and settled down to have my well-earned supper.

I bit into the cheeseburger and glanced over the morning's headlines. More Middle East stuff going on. More city electric rates controversy. I flipped the paper over to see the bottom half of the front page, and there was Dean Caney's picture. The headline beside it said, "Suspect Sought in Second Slaying," and the line above that in smaller type said, "Shooting, theft at Cat Mountain."

CHAPTER 14

The story was short. It must have just broken the night before this edition went to press. In an expensive housing development at Cat Mountain, not far from the Loop 360 bridge where the cops had been dragging the lake for Caney's nonexistent corpse, a man had been found shot to death in his garage. His family, consisting of a wife and two young kids, had been away for three days visiting relatives in Dallas. They returned to find the man very dead in the closed garage and his vehicle missing. From the condition of the body, it was obvious that death had taken place from one to two days earlier. Police, the story went on, were looking for Dean Justus Caney, a suspect in the murder on Wednesday of a south Austin woman. Caney's car had been found abandoned not far from the Cat Mountain crime scene, and reports had been received of a man fitting Caney's description seen driving a vehicle similar to that missing from the second victim's garage. Caney was thought to be headed for San Antonio. He was believed to be armed and was considered extremely dangerous. Almost as a afterthought, at the end of the story, it mentioned another little piece of information. The man who was killed had been a client of Dean Caney's, just like me.

I laid the paper down carefully on the seat of the truck and sat there staring at nothing. Dimly, I registered the fact that my three washers had stopped, their orange lights going out one by one. I ought to get out and go put my clothes in the dryer.

That had been Dean Caney in the red Cherokee, going to San Antonio. Dean Caney with a gun. A gun he'd used to kill some guy so he could steal his Jeep. Dean Caney going to San Antonio where I'd spent the previous afternoon looking for Claudia. Like Dean was supposed to be doing, with the money I gave him. With some poor guy lying dead in a closed garage on Cat Mountain. And the temperature had been in the upper nineties, for two days.

I got out of the truck feeling like a zombie and went into the brightly lit laundromat. I got a wheeled basket and filled it with my clean, wet clothes and rolled it over to the bank of dryers on the back wall. I used two machines and set the temperature a little hotter than usual. I wanted to get out of there.

I felt like my hands must be shaking, but when I stared at them, I didn't see any movement. Still, my nerves were quivering all over my body. With what Lisa'd told me last night about Caney's weird thing for dykes, I felt like he could turn up anywhere and do anything, and now we knew virtually for certain that he was a killer. I'd get these clothes dry, I decided, and go home and lock the doors and windows and call Sgt. Alcorn. After all, this news in the paper was nearly twenty-four hours old. The body of that poor guy had been found last night some time. Soon after that the cops must have started taking me seriously about having seen Dean on the highway. They'd been looking for him all day; maybe they had him already. There was probably nothing for me to be afraid of at all. I'd just keep calm and take care of my washing and find out the latest news from Alcorn, and everything would be all right. I wished I owned a gun. I wished I had a roommate. I wished I'd never thought of looking for Claudia.

I took my clothes out of the dryers still damp and drove home sitting up stiffly at the wheel and looking into every shadow. I didn't see any strange cars parked on Hank Street. My house looked welcoming with the front porch light casting its yellow glow over the lawn and the white floodlights in the back yard lighting up the back part of the driveway and the front of the garage. Only the short section of the drive at the side of the house was dark, the part where I'd ordinarily park this truck. I swung into the drive, and the headlights picked out nothing but the bare stretch of concrete driveway and the narrow strip of flower bed between it and the house. I parked, turned off the engine, and waited a minute, listening.

There was no sound at all, except the faint rustle of the cottonwood leaves from the tree in my neighbors' yard, a sound like rain in the hot summer night. That sound had brought me to look from the window of my bedroom more than once, when I first came to live here. Now it sounded ordinary and peaceful. But would it cover the stealthy sound of footsteps creeping up from the shadows, approaching the cab of my truck? I forced my hand to the door handle and pulled it up. The door opened almost silently. I stepped out of the cab. My moccasined feet made only the faintest scuffing sound as I scooted back to the tailgate and lifted out my sacks of laundry.

I went around to the front door in a hurry. I could be seen there, if anybody tried to grab me. At least, I could if anybody happened to be looking. I hadn't seen a sign of anyone since I got here. I fumbled with the key in the lock a second, then got the door open. It swung inward on darkness. This was the last time I was going out at night without leaving an inside light on. I groped for the switch, found it, and flooded the room with light.

Nothing looked disturbed. I listened. Nothing. And then, from the direction of the kitchen, I heard a small, furtive sound. It was a noise like paper tearing, and it only lasted a split second. I wasn't even sure I'd heard it. I stood stock-still. My heart was slamming against the inside of my chest like it wanted out. *I* wanted out. The door was still open at my back. I was standing there wavering between fight and flight, when the noise came from the kitchen again, this time followed immediately by a heavy thump, like a sack of something hitting the floor. I wheeled and bounded out the front door, stumbling and nearly falling as my right foot caught the top of one of the laundry sacks I'd left on the porch. I staggered forward five or six steps across the grass, trying to recover my balance, terror ringing in my head and my breath coming in shallow gasps. Then I turned to face my pursuer. I had to know what was coming, not be struck down from behind without even seeing my killer.

The screen door had slammed behind me, the wooden door still stood open, and no one was there at all. Hadn't he heard me leave? Was he going out the back door to circle the house in the shadows? What had he been doing in the kitchen to make that noise? It sounded familiar, that little ripping sound. And the heavier thump. It sounded like—

I knew what it was.

I still had the heart rate of an out-of-shape sprinter, but I walked back to the front door and looked in. No one was there. I slipped inside and walked quietly back to the kitchen and turned on the light. Chip glared up defiantly and lashed his tail. The cat food sack lay on the floor with a hole clawed in its side and little brown stars of cat food scattered around it. Pamela watched placidly from her perch on the counter. The accusation in Chip's expression was clear: "You let us run out of chow, and how did we know you'd ever come back? We have to take care of ourselves around here."

Pamela looked up and mewed innocently. "I didn't do it," she clearly said.

"Chip!" I said. "Bad cat!" And then I started laughing and couldn't stop. I sat down in a kitchen chair and laughed until I was out of breath and tears were streaming down my cheeks. After a while I got hold of myself and picked up the cat food. I put a generous scoop in the cats' food bowl and taped up the hole in the sack to keep the rest fresh. I hadn't checked out the rest of the house, but if Dean Caney was lurking in another room listening to me have hysterics, he was probably too scared to tackle an obviously crazy woman. By now he would have climbed out the window and been gone to Mexico.

I did open the closet doors and look under the bed, but of course nobody was there. I got my laundry in from the porch and locked the door, opened the back door and let Ronson in, and then stood looking at the open windows protected only by latched screens. I could at least nail the latches shut; that way nobody could get in just by poking a little hole in the screen and flipping back the latch. Everybody knows how to do that, and in fact there were little holes like that above the latches in two of my screens already. They'd been there when I bought the house, and I'd even used one of them myself when I'd locked myself out one time.

The hammer and nails I needed were, unfortunately, outside, in the back of the garage. I screwed my courage to the sticking place and, taking Ronson with me, I ventured out back. I squeezed down the narrow aisle between the garage wall and the tractor on its trailer and unscrewed the jar of six-penny nails from the underside of the shelf over my workbench. I got the hammer off its hooks on the wall, and Ronson and I got back in the house without having anything horrible happen. I went around to each of the windows and drove two nails beside each of the latches of the screens, bending them over with the hammer and sinking their heads in the wood of the sills. The sills, I noticed, were in need of a good washing. My hands were black by the time I'd finished. Not much protection, I thought as I looked at my new security arrangements, but a little, anyway.

Now to call Alcorn at the cop shop. I went to the phone in the hall and dialed the now-familiar number and asked for Sergeant Alcorn or Sergeant Harris. I was told, "Just a minute," the phone clicked a lot, and an unfamiliar voice said, "Barney."

"Um, Sergeant Barney?" I guessed you called them all "Sergeant."

"Yeah?"

"Uh, my name is Cassandra Milam, and I wanted to talk to Sergeant Alcorn or Sergeant Harris."

"Not here."

"Oh. Do you know when one of them will be in?"

"In the morning, I guess. This isn't their tour. You need something?"

"Uh, well, I just wanted to ask if there's any news about Dean Caney, the man they're looking for, the murder suspect?"

"Yeah, I know who Caney is. You have a personal interest in this?"

"I knew the woman that was killed."

"Well, all I can tell you is what the news people got. We're looking for him."

"Oh. Well, thank you." I hung up, feeling frustrated. All that told me was the bad news that they didn't have an arrest yet. I thought Alcorn or even Harris would have told me more. If there was any more to tell. Caney might be in Mexico by now, and I hoped he was, if the cops weren't going to get him pretty quick.

It was nearly ten-thirty, and I ought to get something done about my laundry before I went to bed. At least I could get it out and see if any of it was too wet to fold. I knew some of the tee shirts wouldn't be quite dry, since I'd been in such a hurry to get them out of the dryer. I toted the bags into the kitchen and started pulling out clothes and folding them at the table.

The house was very quiet. I thought of turning on the radio, but what if it masked the sounds of somebody prowling around? On the other hand, the silence was making me jittery. I went to the phone and dialed Jacko.

The phone rang once, twice, three times. I was beginning to think I wasn't going to get an answer, when there was a click and the background hum on the line changed quality.

"Hi! This is Jacko!"

"Hey, babe, I—"

71

"I can't come to the phone right now, but I'd love to talk to you. If you'll leave your name and number, I'll get back to you as soon as I can." A piercing beep followed. I hung up.

How about that. Now even Jacko was going to be beeping at me when I tried to call her. Damn, I *hate* those machines. I dialed Lisa's number. It rang and rang and rang. I gave up.

What the hell. I didn't have any claim on Lisa Grantly. We were friends, that's all. Just casual friends. Just because we'd been to bed a couple of times, that didn't give me any property rights. Who stays home on Saturday nights, anyway? Besides me? The bar would be packed, women would be courting each other all over town, sitting on Mt. Bonnell admiring the lights of Austin, swimming in the moonlight at Paleface Park, watching television on living room couches, looking into each other's eyes in dormitory rooms—and Cass Milam, stodgy, old unromantic Cass Milam, was hiding in her house with the screens nailed shut, waiting to be murdered.

"God *damn* it!" I said, and started getting dressed for the bar.

CHAPTER 15

The entrance to the Hairpin Turn was through a little vestibule dimly lighted by concealed bulbs, some regular and some red, so that nothing looked its true colors. I crowded in past several couples pushing their way out through the narrow room and passed my three dollars across the counter to the dyke who was keeping the door. She said, "Hi, Cass," and stamped the back of my hand with some kind of design; I looked at it, holding it close to my eyes to try to make it out, but I couldn't tell what it was. I never had been able to figure out one of them yet. They were different every night, I supposed so that nobody could give up bathing and keep getting in for weeks without paying the cover.

I pushed my way through the inner door with its bead curtain and shoved my way through a mass of women who'd chosen that area to stand in and talk. Or shout, actually, because the volume of the music was overwhelming. In the dim, red glow of the bar's lighting, faces looked unnaturally smooth and uniformly colored, kind of like masks. Picking out people and carrying on conversations in the bar takes some getting used to. But there were the heavy smells of beer and cigarette smoke that had meant home away from home to me all my adult life, and I started to relax right away. Looking around for people I knew, I wove and jostled my way through the crowd and made for the bar at the back. Things were really hopping, like they did most Saturday nights. When my Shiner was safely in my hand and my change was in my pocket, I turned around and started scanning the room for Lisa.

I saw several women I knew at tables and on the dance floor, and others kept surfacing and re-submerging in the crowd like fish in a whirlpool. Jacko was there, laughing with a skinny little type with lots of very fluffy, very blonde hair. Jacko had her usual Scotch and water on the table in front of her, and the level was still close to the top of the glass, although even from where I was I could see that most of the ice cubes had melted. Nursing one drink all night was one of Jacko's proudest accomplishments. Unlike some, me included, she didn't ever enjoy being drunk. Instead, she kept her faculties about her and played her girl of the night like a hooked trout, spending her money on Mai Tais or Piña Coladas or whatever the particular evening's prospect wanted to drink. It was money well spent, because Jacko got to know practically everybody new who came into the bar, was almost universally liked, and seldom went home alone if she didn't want to. I caught her eye when she glanced up and gave her a wave. She waved back, but I didn't go over there yet. I hadn't seen Lisa on the dance floor or at any of the tables at this end of the room. Maybe she wasn't here, but I wasn't giving up yet. I started back through the crush, weaving my way around dancers and between and around tables, greeting people every now and then and once in a while stopping to talk a minute.

I found Lisa at a table in a nearly inaccessible, dark, rear corner of the bar, in a kind of ell off the main room where the lights are even dimmer than they are in the rest of the place. She was leaning across the little table with her face about two inches from that of Sharla Doyle, a political-activist type I knew well enough to speak to, but not any more than that. She had about half a dozen beer bottles at her elbow, the red lights reflecting in tiny sparkles off their curves. Sharla had five or six more bottles on her side of the table. The two of them were speaking earnestly and, to me, inaudibly, and gazing into each other's eyes in a way that struck a chill through me. As I forced my way closer through the crowd of chairs, tables, knees, and feet, I could see that they were holding hands across the table top. Both hands. It looked serious.

When I got to the table, I stood there a few seconds to see if they'd notice me. Not a chance. In the general uproar I couldn't hear what they were saying, and I knew I didn't want to. I tapped Lisa on the shoulder—that lovely, lovely shoulder—and said, "Hey."

It took her several seconds to move, to turn her head away from Sharla's as if coming up for air and look up at me. She didn't speak, just looked up inquiringly. She was drunk as a skunk.

"Isn't it about time somebody cleared this table?" I said.

"Cass!" Lisa said in a wondering tone.

"Hello, Sharla," I said. I grinned at them both. It was like lifting the corners of my mouth with a rope and pulley. Hard work. Lisa blinked and smiled vacantly, and Sharla gave me a simpering smirk that had so much condescension in it I wanted to wipe it off her face with a bundle of knuckles. I didn't, of course. I pulled a chair away from the table behind me, ignoring the cries of, "Hey, someone's sitting there," and sat down. I set my beer bottle down on the table, hard. "You-all are a little ahead of me, I see."

"Yeah, Cass, I tried to call you and you weren't home."

"Well, I had some laundry to do." I kept the grin on my face by sheer determination. "I called your place, too, but we must have missed each other. Too bad."

"Yeah, too bad. Uh, gee, Cass, uh, how did your work go? That job? You finish it?"

"Oh, no problem. The only problem is that Dean, I guess you heard, killed some guy at Cat Mountain, and I didn't much feel like staying alone in the house tonight."

"Oh, yeah. I heard about that. Gosh, what do you think it means?"

"Means? I think it means he stole that Jeep I saw him in and went to San Antonio. I think it means he'll kill anybody for just about no reason at all. I think it means I don't exactly feel comfortable knowing this wonderful friend of lesbians knows where I live, since that guy was a client of his and so am I. I think it means the mother-fucking son-of-a-bitch is dangerous as hell and I wish he didn't know what he knows about Claudia, too."

"Cass." Sharla assumed a school teacher tone. "We don't know that he killed anybody. He has a right to a fair trial, just like anyone else. Just because you don't like men—"

My grin was fast becoming nothing more than bared teeth, and I turned them on Sharla. "Oh, yes, Sharla. That's right. 'Men are human beings, too.'"

"Well, they are, Cass."

"Well so was Sandy Marigold, Sharla. And so is that poor woman out at Cat Mountain that found her husband a stinking corpse in a closed garage last night. And so am I, and so is Lisa, and even you are, and this grain-brained bastard is just as willing to blow you away as look at you, so if you want to hop into bed with him just because you think his civil rights are in danger—"

Lisa's hand came down on my arm. "Cassie, it's okay. Don't get so upset. I can see you're upset, but that's not a good way to be. Upset. So don't be, okay, Cassie, huh?"

" 'Cassie,' my ass!" I said, not softly. "Lisa, you're drunk! What the hell is wrong with you, anyway? You never drink beer with me, and then you come in here and—"

"Excuse me, I have to go to the jane," Lisa said with dignity. "Don't go away." She scraped her chair back, tripped over it, and knocked it over, along with four or five beer bottles which her flailing arm swiped against as she tried to keep her balance. I caught her by the arm and managed to keep her from falling. She said, "Whoops! Thank you," and staggered off in the direction of the rest-room. A beer bottle spun lazily on its side on the tabletop

76

until it clinked against one of those left standing and stopped.

I drank my Shiner and wished I had a cigarette. Christ, was I ever going to get over nicotine craving? I hadn't smoked a cigarette in three years, but just let me get in a tight situation and I started reaching for my breast pocket. I drew a deep lungful of everybody else's smoke and sighed it out. Sharla was fussily picking up the overturned beer bottles and setting them upright in a neat group. I drew another deep breath and held it while I ran my hand through my hair and massaged the back of my neck. I let the breath out and reached for Sharla's hand.

"Sharla, I'm a little on edge tonight."

She looked at me, her lips tight with disgust.

"I don't know if Lisa told you, but I seem to be running into Dean everywhere and it really scares the shit out of me."

"Excuse me, Cass. I'm going to get a beer. Tell Lisa I'll be back."

She got up and vanished into the crush, and I sat there. A woman in a fringed shirt and earrings about a foot long came up and flashed me a smile as she took hold of Lisa's chair. "Is anyone using this?" she said as she started to drag it away.

"Yes, they are," I growled as I snatched it back. And then I smiled and added, "Take that one."

"Thanks," she said as she smiled again and went off with Sharla's chair.

Lisa was back from the restroom before I expected her—I guess the lines have improved since they converted the men's restroom to another women's—and she looked a little better. At least she was staying on her feet. "Everything come out all right?" I asked her.

"Cass, why can't I call you Cassie?"

"Why can't I call you Little Lisa?"

She giggled. "I'm not little. I'm as tall as you, you big lug." Her hand came up and brushed my cheek, then dropped heavily to the table.

"And I'm not Cassie. At least, I'm not Cassie when you're crawling all over some broad who has nothing but contempt for me. Lisa, what's wrong? I didn't even think you liked beer."

"Cass, how can you use that kind of language?"

"What kind of language?"

" 'Broad.' And 'Son-va-bitch.' You didn't used to say 'son-va . . . son-va-bitch.' "

This was going nowhere. "Lisa, babe," I said, "Don't you think you've had enough? Why don't you let me take you home now?"

She beamed drunkenly at me. "My place or yours, babycakes?" And she went off into peals of laughter.

A couple of beer bottles arrived on the table between us and Sharla said, "What the fuck happened to my chair? Cass? My chair is gone."

"Oh, my." I looked up at her and showed my teeth. "I guess somebody must have taken it."

Sharla glanced around angrily and, seeing no chair to snatch, had to keep standing. Lisa was craning her head back, turning her face up to Sharla's.

"I'm taking Lisa home now, so you can have our chairs," I told Sharla.

Lisa reached for the fresh beer and gulped down a slug of it. "You can sit on my lap, Sharla," she said.

"Cass," said Sharla in her imperious tone, "Lisa and I were discussing something personal, so if you'll excuse us. . . ."

"Well, la-di-fucking-dah," I said. I chugged my Shiner, pushed back my chair into the lap of somebody at the table behind me, and went to find Jacko.

She was at the table where I'd first seen her, and the level of her Scotch must have gone down at least a third of an inch. You could see the clear layer on top where the ice had melted to water. "Hey, lady!" she called as I came up, and her beautiful, bright, welcoming smile lit up her face. I grinned back. At least there was somebody I could count on.

"Hi, babe. I talked to your machine."

"Oh, you did, did you? Isn't it neat?"

"Well, no I didn't actually. It's neat, though. I hate it, but it's neat."

A waiter came up with a huge, opaque drink with fruit on top balanced on a little round tray, and Jacko paid her for it. "Could you get me another Shiner?" I said, and handed her my empty. She said, "Sure," and moved off deftly through the dancers.

"This is Tina," Jacko told me.

"Hi," I said. "I'm Cass." Tina batted her mascaraed eyes and said, "Hello, Cass," in a voice that would, I knew, melt Jacko's heart like jello on a hot stove.

"What's eating you?" Jacko wanted to know. "You look like a thundercloud."

"Nothing. Lisa's over there drunk," I gestured toward the tables in the dark end of the bar, "and Sharla Doyle is putting the make on her when she ought to be cutting her beer off and seeing that somebody gets her home, and Dean Caney's killed some client of his just to steal his car, and I made a complete fool of myself when I went home tonight, and I feel like knocking somebody's block off, that's all. I just hope some fucking queer-basher tries something when I walk out of here, that's all. Pow!" I swung my fist in a vicious arc that came close to catching the tray with the Shiner on it that the waiter was thrusting toward the table. "Sorry," I said, and paid her.

"Is Lisa really that drunk?"

"She sure is. I was just about to get her out of here when Sharla came back with more beer, and they're off again. I don't know if she drove down here or not, but she sure ought not to try to drive home."

"I saw one of her roommates here a little while ago," Jacko said, looking around at the crowd. "Doesn't Kelley still live over there?"

"Yeah, she does."

"Let me see what I can do." She reached across the table and pinched Tina's cheek. "You two stay here and get to know each other, okay?"

79

"Okay, honey," Tina said. When Jacko was gone, Tina and I sat there and looked at each other. "Are you an old friend of Jacko's?" she asked me.

"Yeah, we go back a long way."

"I've been watching her for a while. She gets around, doesn't she?"

"Uh, yeah, I guess so, a little."

"I notice she's with a new girl just about every time I see her."

"Uh, yeah, well. Everybody likes Jacko."

"I think I like her, too. Does she ever stick to anybody very long?"

"Huh? Oh, sure. I mean—Tina, this is making me kind of uncomfortable, you know? I mean, Jacko's my good friend, and I feel a little funny talking about her like this. I mean, I don't have anything to do with her love life, or. . . ."

Tina laughed. "Relax. I know what she's like; I've asked around among her exes. I just thought you might have another perspective."

"Oh. Well—you mean you're chasing her?" I thought of all those Piña Coladas or whatever they were that Jacko had been buying all night.

"I haven't announced my intentions in so many words, no." Under the mascara, Tina's eyes sparkled. "I think she wants to be the one to do the chasing. Am I right?"

"Yeah, I think you are." I grinned at her. "She likes to be . . . well, she's pretty traditional."

"So am I—to a degree." She winked at me over the rim of her glass. I took a generous slug of Shiner. I'd give a lot to be a fly on the bedroom wall when Jacko the stone butch got this woman home. Come to think of it, I'd give a lot if it were me instead of Tina who Jacko was taking home tonight. I thought of my silent, empty house with its vulnerable windows, and I thought of my sweet and lovely Lisa in the drunken embrace of Sharla Doyle, and my heart turned over with a sickening lurch.

I grabbed the waiter's arm as she went by and offered her my empty Shiner bottle. "Be with you in a sec," she said as she passed.

"What's that you're drinking?" I said to Tina.

"It's a Coral Dawn."

"What? I never heard of it."

"It's kind of like a frozen Tequila Sunrise," she said, pushing the glass toward me. "Try a sip."

I tried a sip. This thing could knock down a lumberjack. "God!" I said and pushed it back at her. "How can you drink those things?"

"I think they're good."

"Yeah, they taste good, but can you ever get up from the table again? How come you're still sitting up in your chair?"

"I'm tougher than I look, Cass," She turned the full force of her smile on me, and I felt just a hint of what it was that had Jacko courting this woman.

"You must be," I told her.

Jacko emerged from the swirl of dancers and swung into her chair, squeezing my arm as she sat. "Everything's okay, Cass. Kelley and Elkhorn are going to take Lisa home and see that she's okay. So don't you worry, all right?"

"Great. Thanks, Jacko." I felt a flood of relief. "What about Sharla?"

She patted my arm. "Elkhorn is engaging Sharla on the dance floor while Kelley gets Lisa out."

I twisted to look at the dancers, and, sure enough, a rather pie-eyed Sharla was clinging heavily to Elkhorn's tall and bony frame as they swayed to the deafening music.

I felt a whole lot happier. At least Lisa was safe for the night, and in the morning was plenty of time to find out how she happened to be guzzling beer with the disgusting Sharla.

If I was still alive in the morning. I looked at Tina sipping her Coral Dawn and at Jacko smiling her sweetest smile across her glass of warm Scotch and water. Obviously they weren't going to be too happy if I suggested we all get together for a slumber party at Jacko's. But what was I going to do? The thought of going home and waiting to be murdered didn't appeal.

By the time the bar was getting ready to close, Jacko and Tina were obviously going to make a night of it. Tina shot me a happy and triumphant look as they were getting up to go. I gulped the last of my beer and followed them out to the parking lot. We stood there for a minute while little groups of dykes from the bar made their way past us to their cars, chatting as if it were an ordinary Saturday night and not one that had a murderer loose in it and big, bad Cass Milam scared to go home alone. Jacko hugged me good night, and I gave her an extra-tight squeeze back. I wished to hell I didn't feel like I was doing everything for the last time.

And in my truck, once I'd maneuvered out of the parking lot and gotten onto the street, I got to thinking how very much I hoped I hadn't held Lisa in my arms for the last time, and it didn't have anything to do with my fear of being butchered before morning. I tried to tell myself that I was just feeling jealous because of Sharla and that Lisa didn't mean anything to me, anyway. It didn't work. I was getting close to falling in love with this woman, too close for comfort. When I thought of what my life would be like if I had a steady lover to obligate me, I flinched. I like my solitary ways. But I also liked that soft, dark hair and that fair, smooth skin and those blue, blue eyes. I liked those arms gripping me and pulling me down so tight against that handsome body that I almost couldn't breathe, and I liked how open and responsive and agile she was when we made love —and now I was thinking of it as making love instead of having sex, and I knew I was getting hooked. "I don't want to be hooked!" I cried aloud. "I don't want to be dead! I don't want to lose you, Lisa!" I pounded my fist on the steering wheel and headed home to Hank Street.

In the darkened neighborhood at two-thirty in the morning my lighted house stood out like a beacon at sea. I'd left every light in the place on and all the shades up so I could see from outside if anybody was in there. Nobody was. After I'd checked the whole house, I took the basket out of my coffee pot and put the dregs of the morning's coffee on to heat. I sat down at my laundry-covered table and scrutinized the bar stamp of the back of my hand. I still couldn't make out what it was. The coffee boiled over suddenly, and I got up and cleaned the stove, washed the pot, and put some fresh coffee in the basket and some more water on to heat. I got out the ironing board and started sprinkling my clothes, waiting for the morning.

CHAPTER 16

When I woke up it was nearly eleven-thirty. I felt a sort of panic when I looked at the clock. I always feel the day's shot if I don't get an early start. I'm just at my best in the mornings.

But I wasn't at my best this morning. I had sand behind my eyelids and my mouth tasted like cotton. I was sore, too, and as stiff as if I'd been at unaccustomed work. Maybe some of it could be from the tractor mowing job yesterday, but I thought it was mostly just from staying so tense for so long. I creaked out of bed and into the bathroom, still trying to straighten up my back.

I did glance into the kitchen and smile, though, as I looked over the neat stacks of clean sheets and towels and underwear on the table and thought of all the beautiful, ironed shirts and pants in the closet. Once I'd gotten started last night, I'd really gone ahead and done the job. I'd used a can and a half of spray starch on my cotton things, and now I had the happy prospect of putting on a really sharp-looking outfit every day for the next week, even to work in. I'd also shined my loafers and oiled my work boots. It had taken a lot to wear me out past caring about being murdered in my bed. I think I'd finally crawled between the sheets at about six A.M., just as daylight was starting to come.

I opened the front door and looked around before stepping outside to pick up the Sunday paper. It was lying under the big eleagnus at the side of the porch.

84

How come they could throw the huge Sunday paper clear up here, when they hardly got the daily one into the end of the driveway? Yet another of life's little mysteries. I picked my way barefooted across the grass and retrieved the paper.

I threw away about twenty pounds of advertising and did a quick search through the residue for any mention of the Dean Caney story. Nothing. Finally, in the back pages of City-State, I found a one-paragraph item that said the police had no new leads and Caney's whereabouts were unknown. Great. Maybe he'd really go drown himself. I was worn out with fear of being murdered, or fear of his finding Claudia and murdering her, or any other kind of fear. I was feeling sort of like I did before I came out to my parents: the consequences just couldn't be worse than the running and hiding.

I lit the burner under the iron skillet and started getting strips of bacon out of the package, when it occurred to me that I might do better to see if Lisa wanted to go out for breakfast. I started to the telephone and then decided, what the hell, I'd just go over there. I'd be harder to turn down in person, and I could see what kind of shape she was in after last night. I'll admit it also flashed through my mind that it would be extra nice to get over there and not find Sharla on the premises. I put on my newly shined loafers over a matching pair of clean socks, brushed my hair back flat on the sides, or as flat as it will go with my curls, and got out of there. I left the lights on in the house. Just in case.

Lisa lived with three other dykes in a big apartment over on Riverside Drive, and the building was one of those huge warrens built to accommodate U.T. students about ten or fifteen years ago. I pulled my truck into a visitors' slot and left it with the windows down. Otherwise it would have been an oven by the time I got back to it.

I rang Lisa's bell and waited, listening to the muffled sounds of footsteps and voices inside. When Kelley opened the door, Elkhorn was right behind her and they were wearing bathing suits under terry cloth jackets, or robes, or whatever you call those short garments with no buttons that come just about to crotch level.

"Hi, Cass," Kelley said. "Lisa's not up yet, but when I looked in there just a minute ago, she was conscious."

"Going to the pool?" I said.

"Barton Springs," Kelley said at the same time that Elkhorn said, "Paleface Park." They pummeled each other on the biceps, laughing.

"Have a good time at Hamilton Pool," I told them.

"Hey, great idea!" Kelley said, while Elkhorn said, "Or Camp Ben! How about going out to Camp Ben!" Their laughter floated on the air behind them.

I padded over the carpet of the big living room in the direction Kelley had indicated and down a short hall to Lisa's door. It was open, and she was lying in her king-sized bed amid a wasteland of rumpled sheets. Her dark hair was tousled on the pillow and her face was pale, the lids closed over those eyes I loved to look into, and she was breathing like she was asleep. I walked up to the bed and stood looking down at her, feeling a kind of tenderness I hadn't felt for a long, long time. All these years of hard work and light love affairs sort of receded and I remembered my sweet and fiery youth, when I thought I'd feel this way about Claudia forever. Love, and making love, and being with my lover had been the most important things in my life. Money had been nothing but a barely necessary evil. A job was something to go to for a few hours of separation that sharpened desire and sweetened reunion, when my hands were not yet the calloused hands of a workman, but still the soft, young hands of a lover. I shook my head violently and said, "Cass, you fool." But I couldn't have told you whether I was a fool for living the way I was or for endangering that way of life by letting romance get a hold on me again. I reached down and touched Lisa's cheek.

"Closing time!" I said cheerfully. "Drink up!"

Lisa groaned mightily, opened her eyes for a second and focused on me, then screwed them closed again and flung herself onto her stomach, head buried in the pillow. Her voice was muffled. "Oh, god, I feel like shit."

"Not too surprising. What were you doing last night, sending an economic aid package to the Schlitz Brewing Company?"

"Oh, god. Cass, Jesus! Don't talk about it."

"Okay, Little Lisa. I won't. Consider it forgotten."

She turned back over and glared at me. "Little Lisa? What does that mean?" Then she remembered and said, "Oh. Oh, hell." She shut her eyes again. "Cass. God, it's all coming back to me." She threw her arm over her face. "I don't know what got into me."

"About a case of Schlitz, if I remember right, and Sharla Doyle, too, for all I know."

"Oh, hell." She took her arm down and looked at me. "Cass, really, I don't know what she was up to. I couldn't get you at home, and I thought I'd go to the bar with Elkhorn and Kelley and call you again from there. And I did call you, but you still weren't there, and then Sharla came up and started buying me beers and giving me all this sob story about her pathetic love life, and I don't know, my mind just flew out the window or something."

"Well, has it come home to roost yet? Because we're going out for breakfast—" She made a gagging sound. "And then I, for one, am going to San Antonio for the afternoon, and if you don't really want to be here when Sharla calls," I watched her flinch and went on, "which I see by your expression she's supposed to, then you're going with me. You can use the fresh air, anyhow."

" 'Who will go with old Cass Milam into San Antonio?' " She struggled to a sitting position and swung her legs off the side of the bed. "Christ! My head!"

"I'll fix some coffee while you get ready." I left her there and went into the kitchen, where I found instant coffee not quite hardened to a lump in a jar. I scraped some out with a spoon, put it and some tap water in a cup, and stuck it in the microwave. Wonderful invention, if you like instant coffee.

I sat at the kitchen table and waited while Lisa ran a lot of water in the bathroom and flushed the toilet and banged into something with a muffled thud and a curse. It wasn't long, though, before she came out looking clean and awake, if still a little washed out and frayed around the edges. She was dressed, too. I gave her an approving look and pushed the coffee cup her way. Now that she was awake, she was looking a little guilty and sheepish. "Well," she said. "What can I say?"

"Don't say nothin'." I gave her a grin. Except that you love me, I thought. Except that you love me.

"So you know about old Ben Milam?" I said.

She drank out of her coffee cup without waiting for it to cool. I don't see how anybody drinks the stuff that hot. "Sure. I took Texas history just like everybody else. Are you related to old Ben?"

"Yep. A genuine collateral descendent of the Hero of San Antonio. He was my great, great uncle, or something like that."

"Did he really say that? 'Who will go with old Ben Milam into San Antonio?' "

"I guess he did. That's what I was always told. And if he hadn't, and they'd left the Mexicans to hold the city, who knows but what we'd all be speaking Spanish right now?"

"Did he realize that, later? How important it had been?"

I shook my head. "He was killed there."

"Oh." She pressed her fingertips to her temples. "Let's go eat. I find the idea repulsive, but I know what's good for me."

We ate in a booth at Steak 'N Eggs. I scarfed down a good mess of sausage and eggs and grits and toast, while Lisa picked at her food and looked green around the gills. I paid the check and we drove out toward I-35. I looked over at Lisa, who now looked a bit more human, and said, "How about it? Are you game for San Antonio?"

"I guess so. It beats the alternative."

"What's the alternative?"

"You guessed it earlier."

"Sharla?"

"She was going to call. I guess I encouraged her or something."

"You weren't exactly fighting her off, the last I saw you."

"Well, you wouldn't have, either, I'll bet, if somebody got you drunk and sweet-talked you the way she was doing me."

I was glad to see her showing some spirit again. "Got you drunk, huh? Just poured those beers right down your throat."

"Well, dammit, Cass, I was scared about Dean and I couldn't get you on the phone, and I did have two or three before she came in. And I'm not used to drinking."

"It'll get you, if you're not used to it."

"Well, anyway, thanks for sending Kelley to my rescue. She practically had to carry me out of there. And then I was sick on the way home and she had to stop the car to let me throw up. And Cass, I remember leaning out of the car door with my head on the curb!" She covered her face with her hands. "When I think of how disgusted I've always been with drunks. . . ."

I reached across and rubbed the point of her shoulder with my knuckles. "Babe, it happens to the best of us," I said. "How did Kelley get you up the stairs?"

She peeked out sideways from behind her hands. "She carried me."

I laughed.

"Under her arm. And when we got up there, she didn't have her door key."

"So what happened?"

"She told me she didn't have it, and I said, 'Don't worry for a minute, dear Kelley. I have mine in my pocket. Just put me down on the floor and get it out.' And she did."

We were both laughing now.

"And then she hauled me in and dumped me in my bed and stripped me, and I couldn't do a thing to help her. And I had on those damn running shoes that are too short for me, and my feet hurt like hell. The last thing I remember was Kelley pulling off those damn shoes. I don't think anything's ever felt better in my life."

"The rewards of a dissolute lifestyle."

"Yeah. And I don't even *like* Sharla." She looked over at me affectionately and we laughed again, and she slid across the seat and snuggled into my side. I got an arm around her and squeezed her against me tight.

"Ain't this the way sweethearts are supposed to ride in their pick-'em-up trucks?" she said.

"Shore is, baby." I nearly bit my tongue to keep from adding, "Wanta get hitched?" Instead, I said, "Just remember, somebody's got to drive this thing. Also, you better get into that seat belt because I don't feel like paying the State of Texas thirty-eight dollars if we get stopped."

We rode along in happy silence for a while, just making little movements now and then, working ourselves up into a state of incredible lust and holding it at a level barely short of intolerable. At this rate I was going to have to pull off into a rest area and do something besides rest, except that I really had no desire to get busted today. I couldn't remember feeling this completely happy for a long time, just bubbling over with it.

We passed the place where I'd seen Dean the other day, and I described again for Lisa what had happened. It didn't seem so scary now, with her with me. "I guess he figured he could leave his car and fake a suicide out on 360 and get the Jeep from that poor client of his," I said. "He must have known where he lived and all."

"Yeah. Cass, if that was him driving by your house the day Sandy was killed. . . ."

"Yeah, I know. That's what upset me so much last night."

"But he's got transportation now. I doubt he's going around systematically bumping off all his clients, don't you?"

"I hope not."

"I hope not, too." Her hand tightened on my thigh. "You be careful, Cass."

A middle-aged man and woman in a new, red Chevy pickup passed us in the inside lane, and the woman stared, said something to the man, and they both turned their heads to look at us. I gave them a friendly wave and a big smile. The man's head snapped around to the front again, but the woman still scowled and stared, and her lips moved. I couldn't make out what she was saying about us, but I could guess. I gave Lisa a kiss.

CHAPTER 17

Caliche Court turned out to be a short, dead-end street, just a block long, with small, frame houses and a lot of cars parked along the sides of the pavement. The street itself was asphalt, or had been at one time, but now it was mostly a mass of holes and white, gravelly dust. The dead grass of the lawns, the scraggly shrubbery next to the houses, the cars, everything was coated with white. My truck raised a thin, white cloud behind it as I drove slowly down the block, looking for the house number Mrs. Polk had given me. Lisa, now sitting decorously in the passenger seat, watched out the right side of the truck as I watched out the left. The first houses had no visible numbers, but then I spotted the number I was looking for, anyway: 618.

The house was little, not any bigger than my house on Hank Street, with a small front porch that had the number on one of its supports in metal letters that had been painted over many times. There was no driveway, but I found a place to work the truck in between two others parked half in the ditch along the road. I turned off the engine and sat a minute, scanning the block to get a feel for the place.

It was a pretty steep comedown from the place on Serna Park Drive. I thought of Claudia living here, and when I did, she appeared in my mind as I remembered her during the later days of our living together in our Hyde Park garage apartment—an anxious frown on her face, distressed and irritable. Maybe this place had made her happier than that. I hoped so. Still, even now I felt a fleeting twinge, thinking how happy I wished she'd been with me.

I looked over at Lisa and found her studying me. I gave her a grin and reached over and slapped my hand down on her leg. "Just seeing a few ghosts," I said. "Let's go."

We got out of the truck, the doors making a double slamming noise as we closed them, kind of neat to hear, when I was used to being alone so much. I waited for her to walk around the truck and we went up the dirt path to the house together. There was no doorbell here, and we didn't need one, anyway, because the door was open and through the torn screen a little girl of obviously Mexican-American extraction was watching us solemnly.

"Hi," I said to her, smiling in my most non-threatening way. "Is your mama home?"

The kid looked at me for a minute in silence, her liquid brown eyes gazing unblinkingly into mine. Then a slow smile spread across her dimpled face. "Yes," she said, putting her hand over her mouth.

"Could you get her for me, please?"

She looked at me, hiding her smile behind her hand, for another long minute. Then she nodded her head up and down. "Yes," she said again. And then she said, "Are you a boy or a girl?"

I gave her a bigger smile. "I'm a girl," I said.

She lowered her hand and let me see her smile again, and her eyes sparkled. Then she turned and ran off into the depths of the house.

"Well!" said Lisa.

I shrugged. "Don't you ever have to deal with that? I get it all the time."

"No, I never have, you butch thing, you."

"Well, you know, kids have certain markers they look for to tell your sex. You know, like men have short hair, or if they have long hair, they have it on their faces too, and men are taller than women, and they wear certain clothes. And women have wide hips and breasts—you know. And here I am with real short hair and men's clothes and wide hips and breasts, and it's kind of confusing to them."

"It ain't confusing to me, baby."

A short, plump woman in an old housedress came to the door and looked inquiringly at us through the screen. The little girl was behind her skirt, peeking around her mother with a mischievous grin.

"Yes? May I help you?" The woman said in accented English. I breathed a mental sigh of relief that I wasn't going to have to conduct this conversation in the baby Spanish which was all of that language I knew. Someday, I thought, I'm going to take conversational Spanish at the community college.

"I used to have a friend who lived here several years ago. . . ."

"Years ago? Live here, in this house?"

"Yes. Claudia Fanding was her name."

"Yes? We live here three years, little more. Before that, I don't know." She shrugged and looked sad.

"Maybe some of the neighbors might know? Somebody who's lived here a long time?"

"Yes, maybe so. This woman—" She opened the screen and thrust out her arm, pointing. "She live here fifteen, twenty years, I think. Maybe more. Ever since this place was new, she live here. Maybe she know your friend." She smiled. "I hope so."

"I hope so, too. Thank you very much." I looked down at the little girl, who had emerged from her hiding place and was once more studying me closely. I waved at her, and she raised a chubby, brown hand and waved, then giggled and covered her mouth. I winked at the sparkling, dark eyes visible above her hand, and she wriggled in response and pulled her mother's skirt in front of her.

"Cute kid," Lisa said as we walked back toward the street.

"Uh-huh. Good looking mama, too." I was looking at the house the woman had pointed out. If I hadn't been looking so hard for house numbers, I'd certainly have noticed it when we first turned onto the block. It was no bigger than most of the other houses, but its paint was fresher and its porch had been enclosed with glass and jalousies. There were green and white striped awnings over the windows, and a mass of bright zinnias bloomed in beds on either side of the dirt path leading to the door. On the side of the porch, strings had been led from stakes in the ground to the eaves, and morning glory vines ran up them, their buds furled shut at this time of the afternoon, but showing the clear color of the Heavenly Blue variety. The grass was as brown as all the rest of it on the street, but, like the rest, it was bermuda, a type which goes dormant in the heat of summer and revives when the weather cools off and it starts to rain again. There were no worn patches in it where the bare dirt showed through, as there were in many of the other yards. I speculated that this meant that no children played there.

Again, there was no doorbell, but this time the opaque glass louvers of the door barred our view of the inside. I knocked on the door frame. Nothing happened. I knocked again, harder, hurting my knuckles. I shook my hand to shake out the pain. Lisa said, "I thought you were so tough." I raised the corner of my lip at her, then dropped it quickly as the door opened.

The woman standing there was old, her hair that pure silver that very dark hair often turns, and her skin was thin and crepey. The hand grasping the edge of the door was blue-veined and large knuckled, but rock-steady, and her eyes looked out through wire-rimmed glasses with a calm and fearless gaze. "Yes? What is it?" she said.

"Ma'am, the lady across the street over there thought you might be able to help me. I'm looking for an old friend who used to live in that house a long time ago. That was the last address I've been able to find for her, and I wondered if you might remember her and her friend. Claudia Fanding and Judy Netsy."

95

"Claudia and Judy?"

"Yes, ma'am. It would have been a long time ago."

"Oh, yes. I remember Claudia and Judy. Claudia was in college, learning to teach retarded children. I admire anyone who can do that."

"Yes, so do I. Claudia was the one I'm trying to trace."

"Were you a college friend of hers?"

"No, high school. We went to school together in Austin. We're both from there."

"How nice! Claudia and Judy moved away just about a year after they came. They moved to be closer to Judy's job. She had gotten some kind of a job—now let me see. . . . I think she was a secretary, wasn't she? A special kind of secretary. Oh, I remember what it was! Data processing. That's what it was. It had to do with card-punching. Like Social Security checks used to be, before they got the new kind."

"Right," I said. "The kind you weren't supposed to fold, spindle, or mutilate." We smiled at each other.

"Yes, that's the kind. Oh, Judy was so happy to get that job. I felt sorry for them, they had so little to get along on, it seemed. Claudia worked at the college, too. But I don't suppose they paid her very much. They called it work-study, I believe."

"Yes, I know how that works."

"They moved to Helotes, if I remember correctly."

"Helotes? That's out northwest of San Antonio, isn't it?"

"Why, yes, dear. It's just a little bump in the road. Though it's been years since I was out that way. When my husband was alive, we used to go out there deer hunting in the fall. It was beautiful country for deer hunting. We always had a contest to see who could get the first deer, or the biggest, or the one with the most points. I used to win about half the time, and he used to win about half the time." She stood for a few seconds looking back at past autumns, then focused on me and Lisa again and smiled warmly. "I know if you go out there somebody will be able to tell you where they lived. As I say, it's only a little bump in the road."

I thanked her and so did Lisa, and she closed her door behind us as we walked away. "I should have told her how nice her flowers looked," I said to Lisa.

"Yes. So bright. Are flowers brighter in San Antonio than in Austin, or is it just my imagination?"

"I wouldn't think they could be, but they look like it. I noticed it when I was down here the other day. I think they must get more rainfall or a longer mild season or something. I'll have to look it up somewhere. I'd love to get that look in Austin."

"You'd get rich."

"Yeah, I would. Do you know where Helotes is exactly?"

"No, I don't." We climbed in the truck which, even with the windows open, must have been a hundred and twenty degrees inside. My starched, creased clothes had wilted long ago. Lisa, however, still managed to look fresh. How some of these women manage it is beyond me. You'd think they didn't sweat at all, but they must. Otherwise, they'd be dead in this heat.

"How about finding some place to get something cool to drink and get in the air-conditioning for a while?" I asked her.

She agreed with alacrity.

"We can take the map inside with us and find Helotes then. I'm going to die if I don't get some liquid down." I cut my eyes in her direction. "How about a beer, Lisa?"

She groaned and slapped at me. I dodged and nearly cracked my skull against the door post. I pulled out, turned around in a wider place at the end of the street, and went looking for a cool spot.

CHAPTER 18

We drove around in the heat for a while looking for some place that didn't look like a bar or a rough local hangout and finally ended up at a Kentucky Fried Chicken. We went in and the ice-cold air felt like heaven. We each got a large Coke and settled with it in a booth. We were the only customers in the place. I spread out the San Antonio map on the table and we looked for Helotes.

It wasn't hard to find, but it didn't look like any bump in the road, either. It must have grown a lot since the old lady had been deer hunting out there, because there were a lot of streets, some in the obvious order of subdivisions. They had names like Limestone Ledge and Chaparral Trail and Roadrunner Circle. Now, if there's one thing I've never seen a roadrunner do, it's circle. They run straight down the road or across the road, and sometimes they take to the air on their stubby wings and glide up over a fence or into the brush, but they're a real straight-line kind of bird. Circle, no. It ought to have been Buzzard Circle. That's what they do.

"It looks like the best way to go is here—" I traced a route with my finger along Culebra to Bandera. "Cross 410 and go straight out Bandera to Helotes. Can't miss it."

"It looks like a long way," Lisa said.

"Are you getting tired? We could go home and I could come back another time."

"No, let's go for it. She looked into my eyes and smiled. "I love getting out of Austin."

"You don't have to work tonight?"

"No, thank god. Off Saturday and Sunday both this week. Then Monday I go on three-to-eleven. She made a face. "My least favorite shift."

"I can see why. Just when everybody else gets off, you go to work."

"Yeah, and by the time I get off and get ready to have fun, everybody else is going to bed."

I gave her a meaningful look. "You don't have to do that alone, you know."

"Casanova Milam! How you talk!"

"Well, seriously, I do seem to be up all hours lately. You should come over."

"Save me a place."

"I'll write you into my schedule. I'll have to disappoint a few others, but that's the breaks."

We folded the map to expose our route and I handed it to Lisa as we walked out into the blast furnace of an afternoon. I stopped and groped in my breast pocket for my sunglasses. "There's another pair in the glove compartment," I told Lisa, and she got them out and put them on.

"Better," she said.

"Okay, navigator, which way?" I stopped at the exit to the parking lot.

"Left, then right at the next street."

We only made a couple of wrong turns before we got on the street we were looking for, and after that it was as simple as it had seemed on the map to find Helotes. You could see right away that this was a little hill country town that had been overtaken by "development." There were a couple of shabby, old stores with deer antlers hanging along the eaves of their porches and with gravel parking lots, and these were cheek-by-jowl with a brand new Lone Star Ice House and a largish shopping center with blinding acres of concrete pavement. There was an Exxon station and a Texaco station and a row of cutesy little shops with wooden false fronts and signs with western-style lettering. Not too pleasant. I pulled in at the Helotes Store, an older place with gas pumps in front and a tin sign on the screen door that said, "Come In, It's Cool Inside," with ice caps drawn on the tops of the letters. We went in.

The place was darkish and dusty-looking inside, but cool, as the sign said. Four men in work clothes were sitting around a little table in the back playing dominoes, and a couple more were standing or leaning against the wall and watching the game. Behind the counter by the door a woman was sitting engrossed in a newspaper. She looked up when we came in.

"Can I help you find something?" Her voice was surprisingly low and resonant, and I looked at her more closely. She had on jeans and a faded work shirt with the sleeves rolled up neatly. Her hair was curly like it might have had a permanent, but short enough to interest me, to suggest a little dykiness there. No lipstick, no makeup. A friendly, direct gaze from eyes which looked straight into mine. I gave her a broad smile of recognition. She returned it.

"We're really not here to buy anything," I said, moving up to the counter and turning my back on the men at the domino table. "I'm trying to find somebody that used to live out here, and I don't have any address for her besides just 'Helotes.' " I filled her in on Claudia's name and Judy's and when they used to live here while she listened attentively.

When I was through, she shook her head. "I can't help you. I haven't been here that long. If I had been, I would have known them. This was the only store out here back then." She glanced out the window. "All that out there is new in about the last five or six years. We're just a part of San Antonio, now."

"I can see that," I said. "So you don't have any idea where I could go from here?" As she shook her head, I had another thought. "Like, for instance, Judy Netsy was supposed to have some kind of data processing or keypunch job and they moved out here to be closer to it. Would you have any idea what that might have been?"

"Let me see. Back then, there wasn't much out here. I don't know if it's been here that long, but there is a data processing service out on Grey Forest Road. It might be that old, I guess. It was here when I came, I know, but I had the idea it was just getting started. Anyway, I'll tell you where it is."

"That would be great! If it's not the one, maybe they'll know where else I can look."

"Can't hurt to go talk to him." She had gotten out a scratch pad and was drawing a little map. "You go right up here about a block and take a left. That's Grey Forest Road. It'll wind all around like this—" She showed me a snakelike line on the pad. "And the place you want is just about three miles, I'd say. It's got a sign, but it's in some brush right where the road makes a sharp curve to the right, so you'll have to go slow and look close. There'll be a little dirt driveway that turns off to the right and goes up the hill. It looks like you're just going off into the woods, but go right on up the hill and the house is at the top." She tore off the slip of paper and handed it to me.

I studied it for a minute to get it clear in my mind, and Lisa, who had been wandering around the store, came up and looked at it over my shoulder.

"But will anybody be there on a Sunday?" I asked.

"Oh, I'll bet so. He lives there, too. John Parker. It's just a small business."

I smiled and thanked her heartily, and she said, "Good luck! I hope you find her!"

Back in the truck again, we drove slowly along until we saw Grey Forest Road. It was marked both with an old wooden sign on a short post and a new metal one with a green background and white letters on top of a tall, metal pipe set in concrete. Typical of Helotes, I thought. The old and new side by side.

I turned right onto Grey Forest Road and started paying a lot of attention to my driving on the narrow, twisting blacktop. The scenery was enough to distract me, true Texas hill country with high, rough hills covered with brushy oaks and cedars, and we caught glimpses of valleys where sheep or cattle were pastured. In about three miles I slowed down and we started looking for the sign that would show us our turnoff. It was really hard to spot in the leafy brush by the road, but we saw it in time to turn into the rutted driveway.

"This really does look like a hunting trail or something," Lisa said.

"Well, that was the sign. Electro-Data Corporation."

"God!" She grabbed the door and hung on as the ruts caught us and the truck lurched and bounced. "Would you come up here to get your data processed?"

"Who knows? I've never had any data."

The house appeared suddenly through the trees, and I pulled up under some live oaks and stopped. A man I assumed was John Parker was sitting in a swing hung from the branch of a big oak by the house, and he got up to meet us as we approached. I told him who I was looking for, and his eyebrows went up almost to his thinning hairline. He turned out to be a real talker.

"Judy must be pretty popular. She worked for me the first year I was out here. I don't know how I'd have gotten this place off the ground without her. Real sharp woman, and a real hard worker. She was out here night and day for weeks at a time, setting everything up and getting orders out on time for me while I was in San Antonio selling our services. A real fine worker. She had a friend that went to St. Mary's, I think it was, and they used to pack a supper and come up here and stay till all hours. Judy would work, and the other one—" He frowned, searching for the name.

"Claudia?"

"That's right, it would have come to me. Claudia would study. I'd just leave them to it and go on to bed, some nights. Judy was a whole lot faster than I was at keypunch." He chuckled. "Of course, now a keypunch machine is an antique. But back then, that's what we had."

"Where did Judy go when she left here? Do you know?"

"Oh, sure. Galveston. She and Claudia both went down there when Claudia finished her school. She'd rounded up a teaching job down there. So Judy went with her. I sure did hate to see her go. I tried to keep her, but she wouldn't stay even for a nice raise. I guess she didn't want to stay alone. Anyway, she went. I wrote a letter of reference for her to a place down there; let me get it. I have it in the file. And I have her home address, too, if you want that."

"That's exactly what I want!"

"I'll get it for you." He got out a ring of keys and went to a door in what was obviously a newish annex to the old ranch house. He unlocked it and disappeared inside, and we drifted over that way and stood by the door. He opened a file drawer and without a moment's hesitation pulled out a folder. "Here you are, if you want to write this down." He pulled a paper out of the folder and held it for me to copy on the back of the map the woman at the store had drawn for me. It had the name of a company, Datamark, Inc., and its address in Galveston, and also a home address for Judy Netsy.

"P-and-a-*half* Street?" I said. What kind of name is P-and-a-half Street?"

"Don't ask me." Parker laughed. "I know I sure would hate to live on it."

"Me, too. I can't believe that's a real street!"

"I guess it is, because that's the address she gave me."

"Well. How weird." I folded the slip, put it in my billfold, and slipped it in my hip pocket. "Thank you so much," I told him. "I hated to interrupt your Sunday, but I was down here and wanted to find out as much as I could before I went back to Austin."

"No trouble at all. I'd already looked that file up yesterday, anyway."

"You had?"

"Yes. A fellow came asking the same questions you're asking. But it wasn't Judy he was looking for, it was her friend, Claudia. He was looking her up for some lawyer. She's supposed to inherit some money and they don't know where she is. I'll bet she'll be surprised when they find her. He didn't say how much it was, but he acted like it was going to be a nice surprise for her. I wish something like that would happen to me!"

I stared at his happy smile and couldn't think of anything to say. The coincidence was just too fantastic. I looked at Lisa, and she was thinking the same thing, I could tell.

"What was the man's name?" she said. "Maybe I know him."

"Oh, I didn't really get his name. He was just some guy working for some lawyer, I guess. Some kind of private detective or something like that. He didn't say anything about himself. Just showed me a picture of Claudia and some girl, asked if I knew her and Judy, and got their address."

"A picture of two women?"

"Yeah. And he asked if she'd gone by Claudia or Marilyn when I knew her. I guess that must have been her middle name."

Marilyn. Caney's old girlfriend's name. I felt sick.

"What was the picture like?" Lisa asked him. "The one of the two women?"

"Oh, just a couple of girls on a beach or a lake or something. One was Claudia and I didn't know the other one."

The two women in the picture from Caney's case file had been standing on a lake shore. It wasn't the picture of Claudia and me this guy was talking about, it was the one of the woman who looked like Claudia, with the other woman that we'd assumed was her lover. I knew now who the Claudia look-alike must be. Marilyn. Caney must think Claudia was Marilyn. He'd called Sandy Marigold 'Marilyn' once. And he'd killed her.

104

Sandy's bloody corpse seemed to float between me and the sun; things went dim for a minute, and I swayed on my feet. Then I was sitting in the swing in the shade and Lisa was kneeling in the dirt and holding my head between my knees.

I tried to sit up, and Lisa said, "Cassie, honey, just keep your head down a minute."

"Don't call me Cassie!" I said.

Lisa drew back looking distressed and said, "Okay."

I reached for her hand and held it and looked up at her. "Sorry, babe. What happened?"

"You nearly fainted. You just started to keel right over."

I straightened up cautiously and leaned back limply in the swing. "Sorry. I just got a shot of vivid imagination there, that's all."

Parker came out of the house carrying a wet towel and a glass of ice water. Lisa took the towel and folded it and put it on my head, and I let her. It felt great.

"Here, take a sip of this." She gave me the glass, not turning it loose until she was sure I wasn't going to drop it. I took a couple of sips and laid my head against the back of the swing again. I felt weak as a kitten.

"I'll be okay," I told Lisa and Parker. "Just let me sit here a minute." I closed my eyes and tried to block out everything but how good the wet towel felt on my forehead. I could hear Lisa and the man talking, but I pretended to myself that what they were saying didn't mean anything. Lisa was telling him about the Austin murders.

In a minute I realized I was going to be better sooner if we got out of there. I opened my eyes, took off the towel, and got up. Lisa wasn't sure I could drive yet, but I said I could. We thanked Parker and got in the truck. It had gotten late while we were talking. I had to turn on my headlights as we wound our way down the rutted driveway. Darkness had already taken over beneath the trees.

Once I was on I-35 and headed for home, I relaxed

a little. I reached over and put my hand on Lisa's leg and gave it a squeeze.

"Are you okay, Cass?" she said. I heard a tenderness in her voice that just melted my heart. I don't usually inspire tenderness — too big and tough, I guess. So I'm especially susceptible to it.

"Yeah, babe. Don't worry. I'm fine. Or as fine as I can be under the circumstances."

"You really think Dean's looking for Claudia?"

"What else am I going to think? He thinks she's Marilyn, obviously. God knows she looks like her, if that's who that is in the picture. That damn bastard must be completely out of his skull."

"He's got to be. Are you stopping for gas?" I was pulling off the expressway and heading for a brightly lit gas station.

"Yep, and a phone. Because if Claudia and Judy are still in Galveston and have a phone, we can warn them."

"Hey, right!"

"And I'm also calling the Austin cops. They ought to know about this right now."

I put gas in the truck and paid for it and got some change, and then we went over to a pair of pay phones on posts at the side of the station. First, I got information for Galveston and found out that there was no listing for either Claudia Fanding or Judy Netsy or any other Fanding or Netsy. Then I put in more money and called the Austin cop shop and got, not Harris or Alcorn, but Sergeant Barney again. I told him the story. He interrupted about twenty times with questions about who Claudia was and who Judy was and what their relationship was and what my relationship to them was and was generally uninterested in my story of the murderous detective, I thought. This guy was just fascinated with all those lesbian details. I got madder and madder. Finally I told him, "Officer Barney—"

"*Sergeant* Barney," he snapped.

"Right. Well, Sergeant Barney, if Claudia Fanding and Judy Netsy are killed before you-all get your butts in gear and check out what I just told you despite your many disrespectful and obnoxious interruptions and insinuations and innuendoes and in-everything elses, you and only you will be responsible and I will personally see to it that every newspaper and television station in the state of Texas finds out about it, and you will not even be able to get a job as a security guard at a fruit stand. And radio stations, don't forget radio stations. I'm telling them, too. I'm—" I turned to Lisa. "I'm talking to a dial tone," I said. I hung up and the phone rang back at once.

"Please deposit an additional one dollar and ninety-five cents on your call to Austin," the operator said.

I hung up.

Chapter 19

I stalked into the station to the accompaniment of the ringing phone. Then conscience got to me, and I turned around and walked out again. Lisa was just picking up the receiver. I took it from her and said, "I'm sorry, operator. We were cut off. How much did you say I should deposit?"

I pushed change into the top of the telephone for a while and satisfied my obligation. Somebody who worked as a phone operator once told me they have to make up bad pay calls out of their own pockets. I made up my mind to call the cops collect next time.

Lisa looked relieved when I paid off the call. "I thought you were going to get in trouble," she said.

I gave her a tired grin. "Who, me? I never have yet." I tapped her affectionately on the shoulder with my fist three or four times and went back into the gas station.

Three minutes later, we were on the road again and I was breaking one of my cardinal rules of driving. I had a cold Schlitz in my hand, and Lisa had one, too.

"After last night, I didn't think I ever wanted to look at a beer again," Lisa said.

"Yeah, but it never works out that way, does it? Doesn't that taste pretty good?"

"After this afternoon, anything would taste good, as long as it was wet and cold."

"How about wet and warm?" I said, looking at her significantly out of the corner of my eye.

"Good lord, Cass. I was worried about you for a while, but I guess you've recovered."

"Come over here." I picked up the remainder of the six-pack from the seat and handed it to her to put on the passenger side as she slid next to me. She put her arm around me on the back of the seat. It felt wonderful. I started to sing like I do when I'm driving alone, really belting out those fine songs. Lisa sat by me and draped her slim-fingered hand over my left shoulder, making little caressing movements with her fingertips over the cloth of my shirt. In my mind, however, was that cold, thick jelly of fear that I tried and tried to dissolve with beer and songs and thoughts of making love with Lisa.

We drank the six-pack fast, finishing just as we got into Austin. I had four and Lisa had two. I stopped by a 7-11 and bought two more six-packs, so I'd have some on hand for a few days. When I drove away, I automatically drove in the direction of Hank Street.

"We're going to your place?" Was that a trace of nervousness I detected in her voice? I looked at Lisa inquiringly.

"I just thought, maybe tonight we could go to my place for a change? Would that be okay?"

"Sure it would, babe. But I need to take care of my animals first. It'll just take a minute."

She smiled and looked relieved. I guessed she didn't want to be in a house Dean Caney might find us in. "That's fine," she said. "It'll be fun to have you over there. It's air-conditioned, for one thing."

"And the bed's bigger."

"That, too."

With all its lights on, my house was probably making the neighbors wonder by now, but what the heck. I can pay my electric bill. Chip and Pamela were impatient, to say the least, when I unlocked the door and came in with Lisa following me. They'd been shut in the house all day because I was afraid I might not get back until late, and now that I was home, I had a woman with me. They knew what that usually meant. Someone other than

109

them was going to get petted. They'll barely even tolerate my petting Ronson. The two cats banged against my legs and ran for the kitchen, demonstrating for this stranger I'd drug in that nobody around here could even count on being fed. I followed them and fed them, gave them fresh water and cleaned the litter box, and went out and fed Ronson and ruffled his hair for a minute. "I'll be gone tonight," I told him, "so guard the house." Then I walked quickly through the house, checking it out. I almost wished I'd find Dean hiding there, because it would mean he wasn't in Galveston on Claudia's trail, or lurking in her house. No one in the closets, though, and the only thing under the bed was dust. I'd been so busy with this thing that I was neglecting my housework. I glanced at the windowsills with their shiny new nails securing the screen latches, remembering how dirty my hands had been when I finished that job. If Caney crawled in one of my windows, he was going to get his hands dirty. But then, he had blood on them already.

I took a lungful of fresh air and tried again to relax. Four beers hadn't done it, but maybe five would, and if that didn't work, maybe some mad, passionate sex with Lisa would. I went to where she was standing by the front door and kissed her for all I was worth. We emerged from it breathing hard. "There," I told her. "That ought to give the neighbors something to think about." We got in the truck and went to her place.

It was about ten o'clock when we got there. Nobody was home but Elkhorn's white cat, Sugar, sleeping on the kitchen table. Sugar greeted us politely and with pronounced disinterest. She was a one-woman type who made a fool of herself with Elkhorn and barely tolerated the rest of the human race. She looked at us appraisingly and then pointedly shut her green eyes. Lisa was putting the six-packs in the refrigerator. I'd meant to leave at least one of them at my place, but I'd forgotten to get them out of the truck. "Give me another one of those," I said.

In Lisa's room, the bed was still in the deplorable

state I'd found it in this morning. While she was in the bathroom, I straightened it up. It just feels so decadent to go to bed in an unmade one. I opened my beer and sat down.

Lisa came in with a beer in her hand, too. We sat side by side on the edge of the bed and drank. I felt kind of awkward. I usually like to be on my home territory. I feel safer there, somehow. But the air-conditioning was nice, and I felt comfortable with Lisa. I shifted and sat on the bed cross-legged and Lisa propped herself up with pillows against the wall, and we talked.

We talked some about Caney, but neither of us wanted to dwell on it right then. We changed the subject to our impressions of San Antonio, we talked about the heat, and we talked about urban growth and its effect on the life of a hill country town like Helotes. Then we drifted into talking about Lisa's childhood — she was from California, it turned out — how she came out to her parents, and what they said and the way all her relatives reacted. But all that time we were talking, that slime of fear was bubbling away down in my mind.

At some point Lisa turned off the light, so there was just the light from the window, from the mercury vapor lights in the parking lot. We sat there in the darkness, and Lisa moved over so that she could stroke my leg with her hand. I leaned back beside her, and we talked some more. And before I realized I was going to do it, I was telling her about Claudia.

I'd given her the bare bones of the story before. Now, with all the beer I'd drunk, the fear of what Caney might do, and the fact of knowing Lisa better than I had when we'd first talked about it, I started letting myself really think about what things were like back then with Claudia and me. I found I was saying things to Lisa I'd never said to anybody else.

I told her what it was like that first time I'd spent the night with Claudia back when we were in high school, long before we'd come out together. How we were lying side by side on our stomachs in her bed, and when she thought I was asleep, Claudia had reached over and patted me gently on the back. There was so much affection, such possession and satisfaction in that gesture that I was nearly drowned in delight. I knew I had a friend at last who really wanted me. It wasn't sexual, really. It was just loving.

I hadn't acknowledged the touch, of course. I was too shy, and I didn't think she'd even wanted me to know about it. But I felt suddenly at peace with myself when she touched me like that, like I was finally coming home after being lost a long time.

And I told Lisa about how Claudia's body had looked then, how I could close my eyes now and see her as she looked at sixteen, her breasts, her belly, the tendons in her ankles and at the backs of her knees, and how her skin had a kind of golden cast all over—not just the tanned parts, but all over where the sun had never touched. I told her how Claudia's eyes had been golden like cat's eyes and how her eyebrows had arched perfectly, and I remembered how I used to run the tip of my finger over her eyebrows and follow their curves and delight in the texture of the hair. And while I was telling Lisa these things, I was remembering a lot more, things I hadn't thought about in years and years. Like the first time Claudia went down on me, how it was awkward figuring out how to position ourselves but so overwhelmingly wonderful that the awkwardness just didn't matter. I thought of the special language we'd invented for the things we did, because we didn't know any words for those things, things we'd never even known people could do. There were no books to guide us or friends we could talk about it with, so we made it our own secret world, all new and full of wonder.

I drank the last swallow of my beer and remembered the time right after we'd come out when we were at her house and her parents had gone out somewhere. She'd promised me a beer out of her father's supply and I'd looked forward to it, an illicit and exciting treat since we were both under drinking age. But before she could get it for me, I'd laid her down on her back on the carpet in the living room and kissed her, and she'd said, "The hell with the beer," with a big smile, looking up at me, and I'd made love to her right there on the rug in her parent's living room and never gotten my beer.

I realized I'd been sitting there not talking for a while, lost in my memories. I was feeling nearly drunk, which surprised me. I think I was just wanting to escape from all the emotion of the day.

Lisa was silent, too, letting me find my way through my thoughts. I sighed. "The last time I saw her," I said, "it was over at that apartment she had with Judy on Rio Grande. Judy was out of town or something, and I'd been drinking all night with some queens I knew, and finally about two in the morning I went over there and knocked on Claudia's door. She was glad to see me, even though we'd had some horrible encounters while we were splitting up. But that had been a while, and we were back on good enough terms, and Lisa, there was just so much there that we couldn't just throw away. We always used to say we'd grown up together, even though we hadn't known each other until we were in high school, because we'd learned everything together about sex and love and getting on in the world. So she invited me in and we sat and talked a little, and then she said she thought I ought to spend the night instead of driving home after all the beer I'd had. Or, no, I think it must have been Scotch back then. More sophisticated, I suppose. So I agreed, and we went to bed. It was summertime, the windows were open, and a breeze was blowing across the room, nice and cool by that time of night. We were naked. We'd always slept naked, so it didn't mean anything, you know. And when I was there in bed beside her, she, who had left me in the nastiest way and who had announced that she not only didn't love me any more, but that she thought now that she never really had—this woman, when she thought I was asleep, reached over and took the top fold of the sheet in her hand like this, and she pulled it up

113

to cover my shoulders. And I knew then that she did care. That she really did care — still cared about me."

I looked over at Lisa, and I saw a tear on her cheek. I took her in my arms and held her against me. "Lisa," I told her, "she was the love of my life. She was my friend, my wife, my fantasy lover made real. Most people never meet their fantasy lover, but I did, and she lived with me and she loved me, and I was a lucky, lucky young dyke. So I've had that. Don't feel sorry for me, because I've had more than a lot of people ever have."

She held me hard, and then she sat up and looked into my face, and I looked into her's. Suddenly the beer, the fear, and all the memories were all too much for me, and I just grabbed her and sobbed and sobbed. Lisa held me and rocked me like a baby.

When I got control of myself, I got up and took my clothes off and lay down again beside Lisa and didn't talk any more for a while. Then she got up and undressed and put her shirt back on without her bra and we got under the covers together. We touched each other a little, just lightly, and then she said, "What are you going to do now?" It was clear from her tone that she meant what was I going to do about Dean Caney and finding Claudia and all that.

I said, "I'm going to take you, Lisa Grantly, and make you feel things you never dreamed you could feel, and make you feel them for so long you'll think you've died and gone to heaven. And then I'm gonna start all over again, because I know you don't have to be at work until three o'clock tomorrow afternoon."

She laughed and tried to poke me in the ribs, and I pinned her on her back and covered her mouth with mine. We didn't get to sleep for a long, long time.

CHAPTER 20

I left Texas 71 for Interstate 10 at Columbus and crossed the Colorado River for the fifth and last time on the way to Galveston. I was sorry to say goodbye to the crooked river that I'd crossed and recrossed all the way from Austin. I wondered how long it would take water that left Austin when I did, gliding in a swift, crystal sheet over the spillway of Longhorn Dam, to meander down the sandbarred river course, ghosting its way between high banks, to mingle finally with the Gulf salt water of Matagorda Bay. My road was straighter and my speed was greater, and I was going to meet the Gulf waters at another place, farther away and maybe more dangerous.

The fear which Lisa's and my rather desperate passion had finally driven out of my mind last night was back in full force this morning and seething in my stomach like something boiling in a pot. I tried not to think about what might be waiting at the end of my road. Instead I went over in my mind the details of the morning. I'd gotten out of Lisa's bed by six. I felt like something the cat had drug in except that I was so satiated with lovemaking that I felt the loose-limbed languor that really good sex leaves with me, even under the tiredness from drinking and too many late nights. Lisa had stumbled out of bed to see me off and to tell me to be careful. She'd said she wished she could go with me, but I didn't even really want her to. This was something I thought I ought to do by myself. I was going to see Claudia. If I didn't find her in Galveston, I was going to go on following her trail until I did find her, as long as it was in range of me and my truck. I might be gone a day, or I might be gone a week. Beyond that time I wouldn't think, for fear that I might envision my whole life stretching out ahead of me in a tedious, despairing search, not for new love, but for old. Dean Caney or I would find her. I was sure of it. I had to find her first.

This morning Lisa would call Sgt. Alcorn and fill him in on what was going on, in case the report of my call last night from San Antonio hadn't made it onto his desk. I knew if I'd called him he'd have ordered me not to interfere with a police investigation by going to Galveston on my own, and I had to go. My friend might get killed because of me, and I couldn't just go on mowing lawns and waiting for the news anymore.

In the lawn mowing department, Cheryll and Larry were doing their thing, keeping up with our regular customers and, even if I wasn't back by then, getting started on a new small-business landscaping job on Wednesday. Cheryll was also feeding Ronson and the cats and bringing in my mail and newspaper. Lisa had promised to drive by my house every day, too, to give the animals some attention and check on things in general. It had felt good to give her my key. I'd called Jacko to tell her what I was up to, but I'd just gotten her answering machine. I'd hung up. Then I'd called back and given the thing Lisa's name and phone number. Lisa could fill Jacko in, and I wouldn't have to deal with the lecture I knew Jacko would have given me about being careful and minding my own business and not risking my life because that's what the cops were paid for, and so on, and so on. Jacko really cared about me, but she was morally certain she knew better than I did how to run my life, sometimes.

I thought about cutting off of I-10 at Sealy and taking Texas 36 down to Rosenburg and eventually catching Texas 6 through La Marque to Galveston to avoid the Houston freeways, but I decided the Houston route would be faster. I wished to hell I'd been able to get a phone number for Claudia and Judy in Galveston. It would have saved me this trip, ended the agony of waiting for Dean to turn up again, and reassured me that the police would be able to get to the two of them before Dean did. Even if I hadn't been able to get them on the phone last night, if I'd had a number for them I could have stopped in a couple of towns as I went and kept trying until I either got hold of them or got to Galveston myself. Instead, for all I knew, they'd moved to Oregon or Louisiana or some other foreign shore, and I wouldn't even be able to pick up their trail in Galveston. But I was sure going to try.

Houston's freeways were probably faster, as I'd figured, than going around the whole, sprawling city, but the time saved wouldn't have been worth it if I hadn't been in such a hurry. I was a nervous wreck by the time I got on the Gulf Freeway going toward Galveston. It about scared me to death the way people drove, cars cutting back and forth across all six lanes in some places, swooping in front of me to catch an exit or just to pick up a little more speed. I'd driven just a little over fifty-five all the way down and much of the traffic had moved right along with me, but in Houston everybody, and I mean everybody, went sixty-five, except the ones that went seventy. I had to keep up or get run over, so I kept up. I wonder how I stood the old seventy mile speed limit, it made me so uncomfortable to go much over the double nickel. Of course in my younger days, I used to break the seventy mile limit by ten or fifteen miles an hour and never think a thing about it. Times change. So do I. I gritted my teeth and held my breath all the way through Houston, pushing my old truck to its best and sitting up straight. I see how somebody could get to like that kind of driving as a sport, but I don't enjoy risking my neck that much out of necessity.

It took a long time to get far enough out of Houston toward Galveston to seem like I was out of the city. The little towns in between seemed to run together. Still, there were some stretches of low, brushy plains with cows grazing here and there, accompanied always by white cattle egrets that eat the bugs the cows stir up in the long grass. I enjoyed seeing them flying across the road in little flocks or standing among the cattle in the fields. Then I started seeing birds I didn't immediately recognize, and it was kind of a shock to realize they were seagulls. And before I knew it, there were salt marshes at the sides of the road, and then salt water with whole subdivisions of houses built on pilings along the shores, and then the highway rose up in a huge arc over what I guessed must be the Intracoastal Canal — at least there were big, powerful-looking boats pushing strings of barges along there — and then luxuriant oleander bushes appeared in the median of the road and I was on Galveston Island.

The smell of the salty breeze through the windows was exciting to old landlubber me. I'd been to Galveston once with my parents when I was so little that the seagulls had scared me with their enormous size, back when the old Galveston Causeway was still being used by highway traffic as well as railroad trains, and we had to wait for the drawbridge while a ship went by. Things had changed from what I remembered, but not too much. There were the same big houses along Broadway, the boulevard that the Gulf Freeway had become. They still had their fascinating second-story entrances with steps going up from their front yards to their high front doors, and there were still the same wooden shutters on the windows against the possibility of the kind of hurricane winds that had torn the city down and killed so many of its people back in 1900. Most of these old houses had withstood a lot of winds and rising tides since then, though I suppose tides didn't enter into it much since the Army Corps of Engineers had built the granite seawall after that storm. Anyway, whatever came, the old houses of Galveston were ready for it. True, a lot of the places looked shabby and dilapidated. It was obvious they'd been made into apartments or rooming houses, but most of them still had their dignity. I remembered Galveston as looking genteelly impoverished, and this part of it still did. I fished out the paper with Judy Netsy's last known address on it and started looking for P 1/2 street.

I still couldn't quite believe there could really be a street named that, but there sure was. I decided that if I lived down here, I'd want to live on Q street, or maybe Q 1/2, since I was *really* queer, queerer than plain old Q. I cruised slowly down P 1/2, looking for Judy's and Claudia's place. I found the address, and it was a laundromat.

The place didn't look all that new, but when I got to looking closer, I could see that it was just dingy, not really old. If there had been a house there where Judy and Claudia had lived, it was long gone now. I pulled into the parking lot of the laundromat and tried to think what to do.

What would Dean Caney have done if he'd gotten this far? The houses in the immediate area didn't look too promising for talking to occupants. The one right by the laundromat on the left was obviously abandoned. Its shutters were all closed and the door was boarded up with plywood that had weathered to a silvery grey. On the right, a big, once-white house, its paint peeling now and its front steps sagging, had a yard full of children's toys and a swing set. From the looks of the toys, the children were mighty little to have a mother that would remember back as far as it looked like I needed somebody to remember. I picked my way through the broken bigwheelers and limbless dolls and went up the steps. At least, I thought, somebody with kids this little is going to be home during the day. I was wrong. Nobody answered my knock.

The houses across the street didn't look any more occupied than the ones on this side, but I went across and tried them, anyway. Nobody home. If I'd been a burglar, I would have had a simple time. There wouldn't have been a single witness around if I'd wanted to break in. On the other hand, these places didn't look like very good pickings for somebody who wanted to steal. They had a poor, almost despairing look. I hoped the neighborhood had changed for the worse since Claudia had lived here. I couldn't imagine why they would have had to live in a place like one of these, since Claudia had a teaching job and Judy probably had something, too. John Parker, the man who she'd worked for in Helotes, had said he'd written her a letter of reference, anyway. I snapped my fingers. I could track them down through their jobs, of course. The schools would be out for the summer, but a data processing place would certainly be open all year. I checked the address her old boss had given me for Datamark, Inc. I wasn't stymied yet. Of course, no good detective would have been. I hoped Dean Caney was turning out to be a lousy detective.

CHAPTER 21

Datamark was in a modern, two-story office building on the fringes of the Strand Historical District, a crowded few blocks swarming with tourists on the sidewalks and cars and busses on the streets. Before I found the place I was looking for I got caught in the tourist section and found it not appealing at all. It looked a little like the pictures I'd seen of the French Quarter in New Orleans. That didn't appeal to me, either. I can stand a crowd in a gay bar, but it's harder on the street where you want to be getting someplace instead of just standing around, and here all these people were gawking at quaint buildings and at each other and looking for quick ways to get parted from their money. It looked like there were plenty of opportunities for that, too. Every restored old building had a ground floor full of little shops with cute names, and maybe an expensive-looking restaurant or two. It never ceases to amaze me how people will spend their time in a place like that when they could be on a beach or in a park, or just peacefully and economically at home reading a good mystery. Come to think of it, though, I seemed to be involved in a mystery myself, and it wasn't nearly as pleasant as reading one. I resolved never to get involved with anything more complicated than the Austin Landscaping Ordinance again.

I pulled into a Customers Only parking place in the Datamark lot and locked up the truck. I didn't like to leave it open in a strange place. Galveston was noticeably cooler than Austin, anyway, though so humid my clothes felt like they were sticking to my skin like a bathing suit. I left the windows cracked a little so maybe it wouldn't get unbearably hot while I was gone. I went up to the Datamark, Inc. front door, took a deep breath of the salty, damp air, and pulled on the door handle.

The reception area I went into had beige carpeting on the floor and chrome and glass end tables at the ends of each of two too-low couches upholstered in a nubbly, neutral-looking fabric. A sliding glass window in the wall on the right had a narrow sill in front of it with a bell to ring. I rang. Then I stood there for what seemed like five minutes but was probably more like one, and a nice-looking woman with big, square, horn-rimmed glasses came up and opened the slide. When she did, a ground swell of noise came out of the inner part of the offices. It was a kind of roar, like some sort of factory heard at a distance, or maybe a gigantic hive of bees. Superimposed on it were the sounds of clicking keys, like an army of electric typewriters all going at once. Obviously Datamark was doing some business.

"Hello. May I help you?" The woman's voice was low-pitched and warm, and clear enough not to get lost in the background. She had a nice smile, too, and I was needing a smile by then.

I smiled back. I wondered what she thought of me, a big, freckled woman with short hair and a man's pants and shirt, standing there on Datamark's beige carpet. I hoped I didn't look as out of place as I felt.

"I hope you can," I said. "I'm looking for an old friend who I think used to work here or maybe still does. Judy Netsy."

The woman frowned slightly in thought. "I seem to remember someone's mentioning a Judy that used to work here before I came. She was a data entry, ah, supervisor, I think." She smiled again. "I'll tell you what. Just let me go see if I can find somebody who was here before me. When did you say she worked here?"

I told her and she vanished into the distant roar, closing the glass behind her and cutting off most of the sound. Now that I was aware of it, I could still hear it faintly, at an almost subliminal level, so soft that it might have been just a noise in my head. I paced around the reception area and looked at an abstract painting on the wall over one of the couches and looked at another one over the other couch and ran my hand over the fabric of the rounded couch cushions. It had a rough texture, but not abrasive. It reminded me of the drapery material Claudia bought one time and made a suit out of, a rakish suit from a Vogue pattern, with a fabric slouch hat that matched it. It had a belted jacket and a skirt, and she wore a man's white dress shirt, stolen from her father, under the jacket. The shirt had French cuffs with cuff links. I thought she looked so sexy in it I could hardly keep my hands off of her. I thought of that now in the Datamark waiting room, and I felt that little catch in my breath that I sometimes did when I let a too-vivid memory of her catch me unaware. I wrenched my thoughts around to Lisa and a couple of the things she and I had done last night. I didn't want to let myself be still in love with Claudia. It would only be with her ghost now, anyway, because the real Claudia would have gone on growing and changing away from me and no doubt would be so different by this time that I'd hardly know her.

The glass slide opened with a little sound that made me look around guiltily, as if the nice woman from Datamark had caught me and read my thoughts. I walked over to the window.

"Good news!" She was smiling broadly now. I don't know what it was about her smile, but it made me feel both welcomed and embarrassed. I found myself wanting to blush and look at my shoes. Instead, I met her eyes with my most direct gaze and smiled back.

"We do have several people here who remember your friend. One of them's just about to go on break, so if you'll wait just a few minutes, she'll come out and talk to you."

123

"Wonderful!"

"It'll just be a few minutes." She closed the slide and vanished again, cutting off once more the beehive sound of what I supposed were computers or something equally mysterious to me. I wasn't a bit sure how data got processed.

After a while the door in the back wall opened, letting out the roaring sound along with a woman about my age, skinny, with a bright print dress in a splashy design and espadrilles. She was olive skinned and dark eyed, with high, arched eyebrows. They reminded me of the high-arched bridge of the Galveston Causeway. With all this flamboyance, though, my general impression of her was of her neatness. Her dress was pressed, her legs were smooth, and her very dark hair was brushed back and held with some kind of mousse or hair spray that kept the strands in place. She looked like somebody who'd work in a place like this. She came toward me holding out her hand. "I'm Ann Miller," she said.

I shook her hand; she had a nice, firm grip. "I'm Cass Milam."

"Velma tells me you're a friend of Judy Netsy's."

"Yes, that's right. She said you worked here when Judy did?"

"Oh, yes. Judy was my supervisor when I first came here. In fact, I got her job when she left."

"Great! When was that?"

"Oh, she worked here until she got married. That would have been, what, six years ago?"

I was stunned. "She got married? I didn't know that."

"Oh, yes. We all kidded her about being a footloose single, and then she up and got married on us. It showed us a thing or two, I'll tell you."

"I'll bet it did. Who did she marry, do you know?"

"Jack . . . what was his name? Jack somebody. Jack Bridger? No, Jack . . . Jack. . . . Rhodes! Jack Rhodes, that was it! I knew it had something to do with roads or bridges

124

or something!" She laughed, and I grinned along with her.

"You wouldn't happen to know where they live, would you?

Still smiling from her joke, she shook her head. "No. I know where Judy used to live, but I'm sure they would have moved. I think she said Jack had a house, but I don't remember where. Wait. I think I remember that it could have been on Bolivar. It seems like it was. But I don't have any idea where over there it would be."

"What's Bolivar?"

"Oh, Bolivar Peninsula. You know, you ride the ferry over there. You've never been over there? You've never been to Galveston before?"

"Not since I was little. How do I get to Bolivar?"

"It's easy. You just get on Broadway, you know, the big street you came in on? And you go to the end of it and there'll be a red light at Seawall Boulevard. You turn left on Seawall and go until you get to a big water slide on the beach on your right. Just past there you'll see a sign that says, 'Ferry Road.' You just take that—it goes off to your left—and get in the ferry line. That's all there is to it."

I was scribbling down the directions while she was giving them, and when I finished writing, I asked her, "How much does this ferry cost?"

"Nothing."

"Nothing?"

"No, it's free. The Highway Department runs it. It's just like a part of Highway 87. If you like boats, you'll get a kick out of it. You can get out of your car and walk around, feed the seagulls, look at the ships—it's a blast."

"Well, that sounds great. Uh, do you happen to re-member the address where Judy lived before she got mar-ried? I mean, actually, she had another friend that I'd like to find, too. Claudia Fanding? Do you remember if she ever mentioned her?"

"Oh, yes, I knew Claudia, too. Or I met her a couple of times; I wouldn't say, 'knew her.' "

125

"Did they live, ah, were they roommates? I thought they were when they moved down here. I just thought maybe I could find Claudia through where they used to live faster than I could hunt Judy down." I paused. "Anyway, like I say, I would like to see her, too. While I'm down here." Why did I feel awkward admitting to this total stranger that I was looking for Claudia as much as Judy? She couldn't read my mind, after all. I gave myself a mental reprimand and an order to act more natural. For all this woman knew, I was Sally Superstraight. Sally Superstraight in a man's shirt and pants and haircut, of course.

"I don't remember the number, but I can tell you how to get there." I got out my notes again and she proceeded with a long string of street names and landmarks ranging from statues in the middle of the street to restored historical buildings to shopping centers to fried chicken places. I wrote frantically.

"Thanks," I told her. "This ought to be a help."

She smiled a quizzical smile, I thought, and said I was welcome and she hoped I'd find my friends. Then she went back into the humming hive and I went back to my truck.

It was like a steam bath in the truck with the temperature outside probably in the high eighties and the humidity surely a hundred percent. I rolled down both windows and sat with the door open for a minute to catch a breeze while I thought about what to do. The first thing would be to get to a phone and try to get a number for Jack Rhodes. I devoutly hoped he'd be listed. If so, I was just about sure it would be the end of my search. If I could get Judy, I was certain I could find Claudia, or at least get a good lead on her. But who would have thought Judy would get married again? How in the hell could she do that to my wonderful, wonderful Claudia? And what had happened to Claudia then? I went looking for a phone.

CHAPTER 22

I found a phone booth—a real, old fashioned one with a door on it that you could close and a little aluminum seat inside—and heaved its tethered directory up onto the shelf. The Galveston directory wasn't near as big as the Austin one, but the humidity had gotten to the pages of this one and they were stiff and curled at the edges, making the book kind of wedge-shaped. I battled with it, forcing the pages over and looking for Rhodes, Jack. There was no Rhodes, Jack. There was a Rhodes, Charlie, and I called him up. He was about eighty, judging from his voice, and he told me he didn't have any relatives in the area. He was the last of them. He'd had seven brothers and outlived them all.

"You know how I've done it? Drink a water glass of whiskey every day and smoke as many Camel cigarettes as I can light. That's the way to do it. Enjoy it. Do what the hell you please. Don't let 'em get to you. They'll tell you cigarettes'll give you cancer. That's all in the mind. Don't you believe a word of it. They'll burn your house down if you smoke 'em in bed, but what the hell? Don't smoke 'em in bed. Can't hurt you then. No, sir, I don't know any Jack Rhodes. Must not be from Galveston, or I'd know him. I was born here, I was raised here, I been a shrimper out of Port of Galveston all my life. Don't do it no more, though. Got to interfering with my smoking and drinking. No other Rhodes left that I know of. No kin to me, anyway. You might as well give up, because you won't find no Jack Rhodes in Galveston. Charlie Rhodes is all there is."

I thanked him and finally got him off the phone. The phone booth was sweltering, even with the door open. I'd hoped for some of the breeze I'd had earlier, but now there wasn't a breath stirring. In fact, the sky had kind of hazed over so the sunlight wasn't so bright, and the air felt heavy and dead. It was probably going to rain. Great.

I leafed through the book looking for a listing for Fanding or Netsy. Nothing. I was stymied. I closed the phone book and let it drop into its slot. Then I pulled it back up again and turned to the back of the book, and sure enough, there were listings for some more towns. Port Bolivar. Crystal Beach. Gilchrist. High Island. I went and got my Texas road map out of the truck and checked it out. Those were all little towns on Bolivar Peninsula. Bingo. I turned to the Port Bolivar listings and started going through my list of names again. No Fanding. No Netsy, but I expected that, since she was married. No Rhodes. I went on to the listing for Crystal Beach with the same results. The same was true for Gilchrist and also High Island. No Luck.

I got in my truck and tried to think. I was hungry, and it was getting on toward four o'clock. I hadn't eaten since breakfast, and I was feeling a little sickish and nervous. I decided I'd get a hamburger someplace and then go to Claudia's and Judy's old neighborhood to see what I could find out. Also, maybe, if Claudia was teaching in Galveston, I might be able to pry some information out of the public schools. It was worth a try, but they were probably not open by now. I went back to the phone booth and looked up the administrative offices of the Galveston I.S.D. The phone rang about fifteen times, and just as I was about to hang up, somebody answered. It was a thin-sounding, woman's voice, scratchy and irritable.

"G.I.S.D.," she said.

"Yes, uh, I'm in town looking for an old friend who used to teach in Galveston, and I don't have an address for her. Is there any way I could find out her address or phone number? I really would hate to miss her while I'm here."

"You say she teaches in Galveston?"

"Yes. Or at least she used to. I suppose she still does."

"I'm sorry, we don't give out personal information over the telephone."

"Can I come in and maybe you could look it up for me?"

"We can't give out personal information on personnel without an authorization from that person."

"Not at all? What about job references?"

"I understood you to say that this was a personal matter."

"Yes. But—"

"I'm sorry. I suggest you visit the school where she teaches after school starts and perhaps you can get in touch with her there."

"But I'm just in town for the day! And I don't know what school she teaches in!"

"We cannot violate the employee's right to privacy by giving out personal information over the telephone."

"Thank you."

"You're welcome."

I hung up. 'School where she teaches,' indeed. How the hell was I supposed to know the school where she taught? I didn't even know if she taught here any more. For all I knew, she might be teaching in Timbuctu by now. I slammed out of the phone booth and drove off looking for someplace to eat.

I got a terrible hamburger with a two-millimeter slice of purple tomato and twenty-three little pieces of wilted lettuce so pale it looked white, all mired in salad dressing on a minute but incredibly tough piece of fried meat. There was a slice of dill pickle with a brown place on one edge, and the whole thing was enclosed in a limp and soggy beige bun. To complement this enchanting entree, I chose a medium Coke. When I tasted it, it was Pepsi. I ate and drank like a starving man. After that I felt a little better. I thought about going back and ordering some fries and some onion rings, but I could imagine what they'd taste like — and look like, too. I passed them up.

By now it was after four and getting on toward five in the afternoon. The rain I was expecting hadn't developed, but the leaden atmosphere hadn't changed, either. I wondered if it was unusual for Galveston not to have a sea breeze. I thought the wind just about always blew on the coast. I noticed that the sea birds I'd seen soaring overhead when I first got to the island were beginning to congregate in thicker crowds, too. I figured they preferred a good breeze to this sultry stillness. Flying in this was probably harder. Maybe they were looking for thermal currents of hot air rising over the land, now. I don't know that much about seagulls, anyway, but I liked having these around. They really reminded me of how far I was from home, and that made me want to get on with the job, so I could get back there.

Following the directions Ann Miller had given me at Datamark was not the easiest thing in the world. Obviously she and I noticed different types of things for landmarks. I kept getting distracted by the huge, bloom-covered oleanders which Galveston is horticulturally famous for, and I'd pass a statue or a shopping center and never notice it was there. Then I'd realize I must have gone wrong somewhere and have to backtrack, reversing that section of the directions in my crowded mind, which was busy worrying about Dean Caney and Claudia and Judy and the problem of finding people who seemed to have vanished off the face of the earth. Needless to say, all this got just a little bit frustrating. In fact, by the time I found the street I wanted, I was having to make a conscious effort to loosen my jaw muscles and breathe normally. I was going to have to talk to some people here, and my temper was too frayed to give me much confidence about not losing it. I parked in front of what

I took to be the house where Claudia and Judy had lived and sat in the truck, feeling the sweat trickling down my back and the sides of my face. I got a paper towel from the roll I keep under the seat and wiped myself down. I took some deep breaths. I ran my hand through my hair and massaged the back of my neck. It didn't make me want to go ring door bells, but it did settle me down enough to do it. I climbed wearily out of the truck and went up the front walk to ring a bell that used to be Claudia's.

Nobody answered, of course. I was tired, and I was discouraged. I didn't seem to be getting along any farther with this investigation. It was hot, and the air felt like a solid weight on my shoulders. The grass here was a sickly green that showed a lack of nitrogen, but still it was obviously growing so fast in this wet climate that no one could keep up with it and the lawns all looked about six inches too high. The ropy-looking, flat seed spikes that St. Augustine grass throws were all over the place. I guess if it stayed this wet it'd be hard to find conditions right to mow it enough. I didn't like it. I hate places that stay too wet to mow. I rang the bell again, then pushed the button about six more times real fast and stalked off.

I glared at the other houses around me. I saw no signs of life at all. This might as well have been a neighborhood after the neutron bomb. All houses and no people. The sky was just a little darker, but I couldn't see any clouds, just that gauzy-looking haze. I was beginning to hate Galveston weather. I wished it were fall. Blue skies and racing, white clouds and a nip in the air. All these scraggly lawns would be magically mowed smooth, and all these closed-up houses would be open and welcoming, each brimming with friendly people just busting to tell me Claudia's address and phone number, and it would be right in the next block, too, instead of someplace I couldn't find with both hands and a road map.

And then a car came up the street slowly and pulled into the driveway of the house across the street.

131

I didn't waste any time getting over there. I was afraid the people would get out of the car and into the house before I could get to them, and then they wouldn't answer the bell or something. A man was driving and a woman was in the passenger seat. I went up to the driver's side of the car and waited as the guy got out.

"Excuse me, sir," I said. "I'm looking for some people who used to live across the street here." How many times have I said that sentence, I thought. It seemed like thousands. "Judy Netsy and Claudia Fanding."

The man, a thinnish young guy in suit pants and a white shirt with a tie whose knot he had already loosened nodded and looked at me inquiringly.

"Do you happen to know how I could get in touch with either one of them? I'm down here from Austin and would sure like to see them while I'm here."

He didn't reply directly to me, but looked across the top of the car to the woman who was just getting out the other door. "Honey, she wants to find Judy and Claudia from across the street."

"They're old friends and I've lost track of them," I said. I didn't want them to think I was a bill collector or anything.

"How nice! I know they'll be glad to see you. Judy got married, you know."

"Yes, so I heard. I believe her husband was a Jack Rhodes?"

"That's right. He and Judy made such a cute couple. She just couldn't take her eyes off of him. And he was so sweet to her. *And* Claudia. They wanted her to be their maid of honor, but she had some family business right then, so she couldn't do it. I know Judy was so disappointed."

"I'm sure she was." Jesus! Poor Claudia. What kind of a creep was this damned Judy, to do that to her? Maid of honor, indeed. I gritted my teeth and smiled with them at the woman across the car top. "Do you know either Claudia's or Judy's address now? Or a phone number? I'd love to see them both, and meet Jack." Yeah, I wanted to meet this prick, all right. In a dark alley. Just show him to me.

The woman looked sad. It was a totally fake look. "Gosh, I never did get Judy's address, but I know it was in Port Bolivar. She quit work so she wouldn't have to ride the ferry over every day. You know how it is at the rush hour, especially in the summertime."

"Uh-huh. Pretty bad. So, ah, you don't know where Claudia went, either?"

"No. Claudia wasn't the most friendly person in the world, at least to me. I always thought there was something kind of strange about her. No offense; I know she was your friend. I guess she just didn't like me or something. But she always seemed so quiet. And she never went out with anybody. I wondered if maybe—" She looked at me with the light of curiosity in her eyes. "I wondered if she might have had some kind of sadness or something in her past. She'd never been married, had she?"

"Yes, she had, too." I stared straight into her eyes. "She'd been married to me."

I never saw anybody's mouth literally drop open before. I got in my truck and drove away.

CHAPTER 23

I wanted a beer and I wanted one bad. I hadn't drunk nearly enough water today, either, and I wanted some of that even more than I wanted the beer. I'm used to drinking gallons when I'm out in the heat, and I hadn't thought to fill the water can on the back of the truck before I left. I pulled into a gas station and filled it now. They had ice there and I bought a sack. I bought a six-pack of Schlitz, in honor of Lisa and because they didn't have Shiner. I put four of the beers in the water can with the ice water to keep cold and stashed the other two on the seat of the truck. I filled up with regular, checked the oil and put in a quart, and glanced at the tires. All okay. I paid up and headed down Broadway for the road to the Bolivar ferry.

I drank ice water out of the plastic cup I carry, and it wasn't Austin water, I can tell you. It had a sort of dusty taste, but it was still wet and just what my body needed. My thoughts drifted back to last night with Lisa and it hit me so sharply that I nearly ran a red light thinking about it.

God, what a fine woman she was! We weren't perfect for each other, maybe, but she was so beautiful and so sweet and so joyfully passionate that I was just knocked off my horse. I did not want a steady lover. No, I didn't. This thing could ruin my lovely, orderly life if I wasn't careful. I caught myself wondering how it would be if she moved in with me. Would she be able to stand the

non-luxurious lifestyle of Hank Street? No air-conditioning, no kingsize bed, no carpets on the floors, no microwave to make her instant coffee in. And would I be able
to stand somebody else there who had a perfect right to
come and go as she pleased, to have her friends in, her
snooty friends like Lucia and Susan? And Sharla. The
thought of Sharla Doyle having the run of my house made
me want to snarl. It didn't seem so good. I'd lived alone
for so long now that I hated the thought of not being
alone in my own house. But Lisa, Lisa! I looked for the
place I was supposed to turn.

Broadway ended at Seawall Boulevard, just like Ann
Miller at Datamark had told me. I got mixed up and nearly
turned too soon, but I saved myself at the last minute
and made a left on Seawall. The street was well-named,
because it ran smack on top of the Galveston seawall.
Right across the sidewalk from where I was driving and
down a few feet was breaking surf.

The Gulf of Mexico looked brown and sullen. The
haze I'd seen in the sky came right down to the water
and blotted out the horizon, so that sea and sky blended
in a darkish muddle toward where the horizon should
have been. Not an inviting scene. Still, the wide sidewalk
was busy with people on roller skates with bright blue
or yellow wheels, other people just walking or standing
and looking out at the water, and even two couples riding
four-wheeled bicycle contraptions obviously rented from
somewhere along the way. There was a broad beach, too,
a little way down from where Broadway came in, and I
could soo various amusement park rides and a lot of
people. I didn't remember much about this from that trip
with my folks when I was so little, and I wished I were
here just to stroll around on the seawall and take it all
in. I spotted the huge water slide that was one of my
landmarks, and then there was a sign saying Ferry Road.
I peeled off to the left, away from the seafront, and went
down a four-lane street that ended pretty soon in a long,
double line of cars, all stopped and with their engines
switched off. This must be the ferry line at rush hour

that bitch who was knocking Claudia had mentioned. I could see why somebody might not want to do this every day, but to me it was exciting.

I cut off my engine and sat there enjoying the rest. It was about the first I'd gotten all day, the first chance just to sit still without a thing to do or a place to go. I drank my beer and thought about opening the other one, but decided against it. I could already feel the first one a little bit, and I wanted my wits about me when I had to drive onto the ferry for the first time. I didn't know what to expect. It couldn't be too hard, or all these people wouldn't be doing it, I guessed. Away down at the front of the lines I saw a cloud of thin, dark smoke go up suddenly and heard a ship's whistle blow once. I craned my neck and looked over the top of the truck in front of me, and I could see a tall shape that must be the end-on view of the ferry boat. It seemed to be going away from me, but then the cars ahead of me started up and I started my truck to be ready, and the line began to move. Another boat was docked to the left of where I'd spotted the first one, and it was this one that we were being loaded onto now. I didn't get much chance to study the boat before I was driving across a rumbling metal ramp and onto an asphalt-paved deck marked with lanes like a highway, and a woman with a big signal flashlight like you see police use to direct traffic at accident scenes was motioning me to hurry up and pull right behind the truck I'd followed onto the boat. She had me come up real close to him and stop. There was a sign saying to stop engine and set brakes, so I did that. I breathed a sigh of relief.

The boat was huge. I'd pictured something that might hold five or six cars, but this thing was way bigger than that. I think there must have been more like fifty or sixty cars on it, at least. I could feel the deck tilt slightly when they were loading cars onto the side I was on. It had been leaning a little to the left from the weight of the ones that had been ahead of me in the lines and had gotten on the other side. It was a new experience, sitting in my truck and feeling the road move under me.

In the middle of the boat, running along the same directions as the traffic lanes, was a big, high superstructure with a pilot house sticking up at each end. I could see that, instead of turning the boat around, the pilot had only to walk from one end to the other. There were stairs going up to the higher level, and I got out of my truck and walked up to them. Just then an enormous blast of the boat's horn made me jump, the engines rumbled, vibrating the deck under my feet, and the pilings started sliding along beside the rail. We were moving.

I abandoned the idea of going upstairs and instead followed a crowd of touristy-looking people up to the front of the boat. You could stand right at the front with only a rusty chain between you and the muddy salt water. Seagulls were flapping all around, close to our heads, calling like laughter. A woman and a kid were throwing pieces of bread into the air, and the gulls were swooping and catching it before it could fall. It was fascinating.

I watched a while, and then some big ships caught my attention, two of them, riding very high in the water with anchor cables running as straight as bars from their bows to the surface of the water. I walked around a little, climbed the steep, narrow stairs to the high upper deck, and stood on the little balcony just below the windows of the pilot house, right under the name of the boat painted there: Gib Gilchrist. From up here you could really see far. I spotted a lighthouse, black and very tall, on the shore we were approaching. It had shown up on my map as Port Bolivar Lighthouse. If Judy Netsy Rhodes was still in Port Bolivar, I was going to find her, and it was going to be in the next hour.

We got to the other side and the ferry docked with only a slight jostling against the big bundles of pilings that stood close along either side of the boat. The deck hands took down the chain at the front of the boat and got ready to adjust the metal ramp so we could drive off, and I went back and got in my truck. Before I knew it, I was signaled to drive off and I did. No sweat. I was on Bolivar Peninsula. I saw a sign that pointed to Port Bolivar and I took the road to the left.

The narrow blacktop road ran through marshy-looking fields without much sign of human habitation. There were a few cattle and their accompanying egrets, and I saw a big, white bird I thought must have been a heron standing in the water at the edge of a pool by the road. The sky had never lost that haze and now was showing signs of premature darkness. There was still no breeze, so that it seemed like my truck and me were the only things moving in the landscape. I felt like I was in an alien world. I was a long way from Austin.

Port Bolivar wasn't much more than a village. I guess that's what it was, really, a fishing village. I saw boats that I supposed were shrimp boats tied up along its waterfront, and there were a few bigger ones, too, with names like Amoco Seaserve that told me they probably worked with the offshore oil rigs. There were warehouses and shrimp-buying companies along the docks, too. I wondered what Judy Netsy's husband did for a living in this little town. Maybe he was a shrimper, like old Charlie Rhodes in Galveston. But then surely Charlie would have known him, wouldn't he? I looked for a pay phone. When I found one outside a little store, I called directory assistance and asked for a listing for Jack Rhodes.

"I'm sorry," the operator told me. That number is unpublished."

WHOOPEE! So Jack Rhodes really existed, and he had a phone!

"Operator," I told her, "this is an emergency. I have to get in touch with Mrs. Jack Rhodes immediately. There must be some way you can help me."

"I'm sorry, sir, but I'm not allowed to give out an unpublished number."

"But this is an emergency!"

"Is it a matter of life and death?"

I took a breath. "Yes," I said, really believing it in its enormity for the first time. "It's a matter of life and death. That's exactly what it is."

"I'm not authorized to help you." She sounded like she was weakening a little.

"May I speak to the chief operator, then, please?" I'd just remembered the woman I used to know who worked for the phone company had said something about a situation like this. You had to go through the chief operator.

"Certainly, ma'am. One moment, please." She sounded relieved to be off the hook. Also, she'd finally gotten my gender right. Anyway, being sirred over the phone isn't as bad as being sirred in person. Less embarrassing for all concerned. The chief operator came on and identified herself. I repeated what I wanted, and she said, "This is a life-and-death emergency?"

"Yes, ma'am, it is."

"I'll ring the party and ask if they wish to speak to you. If you'll give me your name and number, I'll have them call you back if they wish."

I told her my name and read off the number stamped faintly on the phone and hung up and waited. And waited. It must have been five minutes later that the phone finally rang. I'd been pacing back and forth in front of it, and now I wheeled and grabbed the receiver on the first ring.

"Hello?" My voice sounded thin and squeaky.

"Hello, Cass? This is Judy."

I almost cried. "Judy, I have to see you and it's real important. Can I come over?"

"I guess so. What's it about?" She sounded wary.

"I'll tell you the whole story when I get there. How do I find your place from a little store about a block from some fishing boats in Port Bolivar?"

She gave me directions, and they were simple, for a change. I followed the road down four blocks, turned right, and there was the brick house Judy had described, with the yellow porch light shining in the gathering dusk to light my way. I parked the truck in the driveway and got out shaking with relief. Judy opened the door before I got to it and looked me up and down and then, finally, smiled.

"Cass, it's good to see you." She stood aside and let me in, and I walked into a homey and comfortable living room. She sat in a big, stuffed chair and I sat on the edge of the couch and we looked at each other.

She was older and thinner than I remembered, and she had a lot of lines in her face that hadn't been there when I last saw her, but then I guess I did, too. She was still unmistakably Judy.

"What's going on?" she said.

"Judy, I hired a man to look for Claudia for me and now I find out he's a killer. And I think he's still looking for her. I think he's crazy, and I know he was trying to trace her through you. I came to warn you and try to beat him to Claudia, if you know where she is."

Judy stared at me with a strange look on her face. "I think he already found me."

"Oh, god. He was here?"

"Yes. He was here last night. He seemed nice enough, so I talked to him and he went away, that's all."

"You told him where Claudia is?"

Judy stared at her hands in her lap and didn't answer. I waited as long as I could, but I had to know. "Judy?" I said.

She looked up at me and I saw the sorrow on her face, but still, the words, when they came, were almost too much to bear.

"Cass," Judy said, "Claudia's dead."

CHAPTER 24

Outside, a sudden gust of wind moaned through the salt cedars around the house. Silence followed it, but only for a moment. Then another gust came, not as violent, but lasting longer. I could feel them in my heart. Judy said nothing else, and neither did I. There was nothing to say, nothing to think, not even much to feel. I thought, "I should cry." But I didn't. Finally I took a deep breath and sighed.

"How?" I said.

"She had anemia. Pernicious anemia."

"I didn't know people died from anemia."

"Yes, they do."

"Oh."

I sat there and looked at the carpet. There were several little pieces of thread on the carpet by the couch. Judy must have been doing some sewing. Claudia used to sew a lot. I used to have to pick up little threads like that from the floor when she did.

"I'm sorry, Cass."

I nodded.

"I thought about calling you, but it had been so long."

I nodded again.

"I didn't know how to get you. Your address or anything."

The wind was steadying outside, a low moan rising and falling in the cedar trees, rising and falling and never quite dying away.

141

"Can I make you some coffee?"

"Yes," I said. "That would be good."

She got up and went into another room. It was pitch dark outside the windows now. Rain was starting to whip in little volleys like rifle fire across the glass. I wondered if it was going to be a real storm. I didn't care much one way or the other. I wondered where Judy's husband was. He was going to get wet coming in.

Judy came back and set a cup of coffee in a saucer on the end table by the couch. "Would you like anything in that?" she said.

"No. Thank you. Black's just fine."

"Sounds like we're going to get part of that storm, after all."

"What storm?"

"That hurricane out there. Haven't you been listening to the radio?"

I shook my head.

"It's just one of those little ones that come up suddenly right off shore. It started just this morning."

"I didn't know about it."

"Oh, it's not even supposed to come in here. I think they said it was coming in around Beaumont. That puts us on the good side of it. I don't think it's anything to worry about."

"Good."

I picked up the coffee and drank. It was way too hot, but I didn't care. I didn't seem to be feeling much.

"Cass, are you going back tonight? You still live in Austin, don't you, or have you moved?"

"No, I still live there."

"If you're going back tonight, we'd better check the weather report. You don't want to be out driving in this if it gets bad."

"I'll be okay."

"Or you could stay here, if you like. My husband's out of town, so I'm on my own."

"No, thanks. Judy, was it bad for her? I mean, was

there any . . . any pain or anything? I don't know anything about that disease."

"Cass, I didn't even know about it until right at the last. You know, we weren't seeing much of each other." She paused and sipped her coffee. "She didn't call me until she was in the hospital for the last time. And then she wouldn't talk about it, really. She just wanted me to handle the . . . the arrangements. The house, her things. The funeral and all."

"What about her parents?"

"They didn't really . . . I know they really cared about her, but. . . ."

"They just let her die down here alone, huh?"

"Well, you know how they felt about her . . . her, ah, lifestyle. You know how religious they are, and. . . ." Her words trailed off into silence. I sat listening to the wind and the rain squalls that lashed the windows.

"Why did you leave her, Judy?"

"Well, Cass, I'm . . . I really wasn't . . . I'm not a lesbian."

"I guess you fooled us all, huh?"

"I loved her, Cass. I really did. But I just couldn't stand all the, you know, all the pressure, I guess. All the, I don't know. All the disapproval, I guess I mean. And I do like men, Cass. I really do."

"Well."

"They came to her funeral, Cass. Her mother and father."

"Huh."

I drank my coffee.

"She's buried in a little cemetery here, if you wanted to know. We bought her a little stone. You could see, if you wanted to."

"Where is it?"

She gave me directions. I didn't write them down. I'd remember them. I got up and walked to the door. Judy followed me.

"Cass."

143

I looked at her.

"I should have called you, I know. I just didn't, that's all. I didn't know she'd still mean anything to you. And I thought you'd have a new life by now; you might not want to be reminded."

"It's okay, Judy. Thank you for taking care of things."

"Be careful in this weather."

"I will. Thanks." I went out into the storm. The wind was coming in pretty hard gusts, making the small rain sting when it lashed across my bare arms and face. I turned the truck around, seeing the cedars bowing and rising ponderously in the sweep of the headlights. I headed back up the road and took the turnoff for the Port Bolivar Cemetery.

It was a narrow road, not paved but topped with crushed white shell. Oyster shell, I guess it was. Enough rain had already fallen for the road surface to yield a little beneath my truck wheels. The cemetery was about a mile away from Judy's house. I found it with no trouble, stopped the truck outside the gate, and got out.

The storm was showing signs of dying down. The wind was steady now, but the hard gusts were going, and the rain was reduced to a light sprinkle, blown by the wind but no longer stinging my skin. It looked like Judy had been right in not being afraid of the hurricane. I walked up the little two-rut road through the cemetery and counted the rows of graves as I went. I was looking for the eighth row from the front. I found it and turned down it, walking slowly and shining my emergency flashlight on the headstones. Claudia's was nearly at the end of the row, not far from the fence.

"Claudia Jane Fanding," it said in small, neat letters. Her birthdate was there, and the date of her death, nearly three years ago. The stone was quite small, and there was no other inscription. I switched off the flashlight and stood there in the last of the rain.

I don't know how long I stood. I tried to think of something to say, but nothing came to me, just emptiness. I remembered passing a big cemetery in Galveston this afternoon, one with rows of huge statues and monuments, hundreds of them. I wished she'd been buried there, with a big obelisk over her grave with some verses on it or something, instead of out here in the dark by the Intracoastal Canal — by herself with such a little stone, where nobody ever came. I wished I could have known about it; I could have had them put something on her stone. There ought to be something, at least. Some lines of poetry or something, something so people that came along would know she'd been a person worth something, a person somebody loved. A fine lesbian. A brave, tough, loving lesbian. My lover. Not just somebody who was born and lived thirty-four years and died. I'm thirty-eight. Now Claudia would never be as old as I am. All this time I'd thought she was just a year behind me, but now she was four years behind and she'd never get any closer. When I was eighty, she'd still be thirty-four. She was never going to come back and knock on my door on Hank Street like I'd always hoped maybe she would. I was never going to open my door and see her standing there looking older but the same, smiling hopefully at me and saying, "Cassie, I came home."

I stood there in the dark, in the salt-smelling air, more alone than I think I'd ever been. I wanted her to know I'd come at last; I'd finally gotten here. "Claudie?" I said. "It's me, Cassie." And then the tears came, and I crouched on my knees in the mud and the scraggly, short grass of her grave and cried so hard I felt like I'd tear in two.

A long time later I got up and walked back to the truck at the cemetery gate. I got behind the wheel, but I didn't reach for the key. I sat there in the dark. My throat hurt. I couldn't think, and I didn't want to. I knew I ought to go home, but I couldn't just drive off and leave her alone back there forever. I felt the can of Schlitz on the seat where it had been all afternoon since I bought it at the gas station in Galveston, and I opened it and drank. It was warm and strong going down my throat, and it tasted good. I finished the beer, and then I curled up against the door in my muddy clothes and slept.

I woke up once from a nightmare of falling. The wind had risen again, and the rain was starting to come down hard. I shifted cramped muscles and slept again. I woke once again during a lull in the storm and got out and peed beside the truck. I got back in and thought of driving home. Instead, I curled up again in the corner behind the wheel and dropped into exhausted, troubled dreams. Claudia was sitting in the truck with me, and we were on the ferry at night. The deck was moving beneath us, and Claudia said, "But what about Lisa?" and I said, "She calls me Cassie, too," and she started to cry. I woke up to the truck's rocking in a wind that was blowing hard.

I'd never known a wind to blow so hard. The sound of it was huge, a deep, keening roar that almost drowned out thought. Well, I said to myself, I've done it now. I could bet the ferry wasn't going to be running in this, and in fact I'd be lucky to hold the truck on the road in it. If this was the good side of a little hurricane, I was sure as hell glad I'd never seen the bad side of a big one. I stretched painfully and tried moving my legs, which were almost locked with stiffness from sleeping the way I had. It hurt me in every joint to move. Logic told me the only thing to do was go back to Judy's and beg for shelter. She'd take me in, all right. I tried to remember how long it took one of these storms to clear the coast. It didn't seem to me like they lasted very long. They just moved inland and died out in a lot of rain, as I recalled. I wished I knew more about what to expect. Anyway, I was probably stuck on Bolivar for the night.

I started the truck and put it in gear, and then I still couldn't just drive off. I got out into the hurricane and fought my way back up the little road. I had to say good-bye one last time.

I literally had to lean against the wind. The effort it took to put one foot in front of the other was surprising, and my feet kept slipping in the mud. If the wind had suddenly dropped, I would have fallen flat on my face.

It didn't drop. It increased, if anything, moment by moment. The rain was so heavy it was like trying to breathe under water. I was soaked the instant I got out of the truck, and my wet shirt flapped behind me violently, whipping the skin raw on my back.

I got to Claudia's grave and stopped—barely able, against the wind and the rain, to keep my eyes open enough to see in the dark the little stone that was my lover's only monument. I got down on my hands and knees over her grave the way I used to over her body in life so long ago. I was crying again, but not the rough, tearing sobs I'd cried before. Now I just felt a deep, hopeless sorrow. I didn't try to speak; the wind would have torn the words away, facing it the way I was.

I struggled to my feet at last. I couldn't say goodbye to her now, any more than I ever had. I'd always have her with me a little, I guessed. But now I knew I could never hope any more to see her standing at my door. We'd said our last goodbye years ago.

I turned back toward the truck, staggering under the force of the wind, and Dean Caney was standing not ten feet away, his legs braced wide apart against the storm and a piece of iron pipe in his hand.

CHAPTER 25

In the dark and the rain he didn't look like he had in his office in Austin, but it was Dean, all right. His clothes were plastered to his body like mine, outlining his hulking form against the lighter shapes of the gravestones behind him. He was between me and my truck.

Neither of us moved for several seconds. I couldn't take my eyes off of him. This was the killer I'd been running from in Austin and racing with to find Claudia, and now here we were at the end of the race. The piece of pipe in his hand told me I was going to be the next victim, that in a few minutes I'd be a bloody, battered corpse like poor Sandy, lying in the mud by the Intracoastal Canal with the hurricane rains pouring over me and washing my blood into the soggy ground. I could see that picture so clearly for a minute that I groaned aloud. The wind whipped the sound away. I didn't see how I could run from him in the storm; I'd barely been able to walk in it. I wasn't going to stand here and die, either. I was going to have to fight. Looking at this man who'd killed two people and who would have killed my Claudia if he could, I felt an overpowering surge of fury.

"God damn you, you bastard!" I shouted at him. "God damn you to hell!"

I don't know if he could hear me over the noise of the storm. His mouth moved, though. I couldn't catch all the words, but the last one was "dyke." He took a step toward me, keeping his legs wide apart for balance in the wind.

I took a step backward and felt my foot slip a sickening inch or so and then stop against some irregularity in the ground. If I fell, I was a dead woman. We stopped for the space of a breath or two, still facing each other.

"Dyke, I'll kill you," Dean shouted. "I'll kill you! I'll kill you! I'll kill you!" Slowly, he began raising the pipe in his hand. He stepped carefully toward me again.

"Dean, why?" I yelled as loudly as I could, trying to get him to talk to me, stall him, give me time to think.

"You fucking dyke, you made me kill—" I didn't catch the last word, but I thought it must have been "Sandy."

"Why, Dean?" It was hard enough just to get air into my lungs in the sheeting rain and the solid wall of wind, and yelling into it took all the effort I could make. My throat felt raw.

"I loved her, and you made me kill her. God damn you, god damn you, dyke! Kill you, god damn you!" He took another step. I stepped back as he did. My heel caught the corner of Claudia's headstone, my left foot slipped in the mud, and my leg shot out from under me. I fell heavily on my left shoulder, pain stabbing up through the joint from the point of impact. I kicked backward with both legs and rolled to the left, onto my hands and knees, and scrambled behind the big granite marker of the next grave. I grabbed hold of the top of the stone and yanked myself to my feet, feeling the skin of my palm tear as it scraped hard along the rough top of the granite. Dean was three feet away, just on the other side of the stone, the pipe rising high over his head. I saw it pause and start its downward swing, and I ducked and heard, even over the storm, the thudding clang as it smashed into the granite above my head. That must have hurt his hands like hell. Good. I scrambled away again, using my hands and feet, running upright a step of two, half-falling and catching myself with my hands and arms, pushing myself upright and running again. And I hit the barbed wire fence that surrounded the cemetery.

My momentum was so great that the impact with the tightly stretched wires threw me to the ground. I could see Dean's feet inches away from my eyes as my head hit the mud, and I knew that the pipe was coming down. I kicked out and rolled away under the fence. I heard the singing twang as the pipe came down with tremendous force and caught the top strand of the fence wire, and almost at the same time there was a shriek of pain or anger from Dean. I didn't know what he'd done to himself and I didn't wait to find out. I had to get to my truck and get out of there. I was up like a jackrabbit, but I tried to move too fast and the wind caught me and threw me bodily down in the mud again. I was almost stunned by the impact; I'd fallen without being able to catch myself at all and hit hard. But I was operating on pure terror now, and I was up and running again as I saw Dean coming over the fence.

Which way was the truck? I was disoriented and half-blinded by the rain and the mud in my eyes. I dashed a frantic hand across my face, trying to clear my vision. Instead of the truck, all I saw was a small shed, like a tractor shed, about twenty yards away and a dark wall of some kind of vegetation leading away from it into the darkness. I ran for that, slipping and stumbling. It almost seemed like I was moving in slow motion; the shed and the hedge or whatever it was weren't getting any closer, and Dean was dashing wildly up to cut off my escape that way. I bore off to try to get around him, though whether the bushes and the shed were going to give me any hope if I reached them I didn't know. I was gaining a little, I thought. Dean seemed to be favoring one leg as he ran. He must have hurt himself back at the fence. I redoubled my effort in a desperate, last dash toward possible safety, and then I was running on nothing. My feet, instead of meeting rough ground and slippery mud, were plunging through the air, and then warm, surging water closed over me with a tremendous splash.

I went under for what seemed like six feet, and may have really been that. I took in a great lungful of water as I went down, before I could realize what had happened and hold my breath. The scalding pain of salt in my throat and nose and in the raw, scraped places on what seemed like practically every other part of my body seared me like hot irons. I thought I was dying, but then my feet felt the soft ooze of the bottom and sank deep in it. I let my knees bend as my feet sank, and when I felt the solid resistance of the true bottom under my shoes, I pushed upward as hard as I could.

It was a mistake.

My head shot up and cleared the surface of the water completely, and blurred vision revealed the silhouette of Dean Caney standing spread-legged on the bank waiting for me, the pipe poised above his head in both hands. I spluttered out water and gasped in air as I saw Dean's head jerk in my direction. I coughed and choked and went under again and fought my way up again, and as soon as my face was out of the water I yelled, "Dean, help! I can't swim!" I went under again and swam like the devil. I got out a good bit farther from the bank and came up again, splashing mightily and shouting, "Help!" at the top of my lungs. I got a real good breath this time and dived again, swimming underwater parallel to the bank of what I now realized was the Intracoastal Canal itself, which accounted for the depth and the steep drop-off right at the bank. A natural pond wouldn't have been deep enough that close to shore to have saved me. I barely surfaced for air and dived and swam again, in the direction I thought the shed and the bushy hedge ought to be. Finally I surfaced cautiously and looked around. It was hard to see in the rain-drenched darkness, and the waves the wind was kicking up, even here in the canal, were throwing me around a lot. They were to my advantage, though, because I knew they'd make me hard to spot from the bank. I was about ten yards off the shore of the canal and just opposite the shed. Dean was a good hundred feet away, looking in the other direction. Keeping low in the water, I swam for the bank.

It was really steep. Once I reached it, I tried to pull myself out by grabbing hold of the clumps of salt grass that hung over the edge, but the sharp-edged blades sliced into the palm of the hand that I'd already hurt, so that I practically screamed. I treaded water under the overhang of the bank and tried to collect my courage to grab that grass and haul myself out in spite of the pain. I was just about at the fag end of my strength, and I could see myself drowning here quite easily. It was all I could do to keep moving my legs and hands enough to keep my face out of water. I began to doubt that, pain or no pain, I had the strength left to pull myself out of that canal.

I waited another minute or so, hoping like anything that Dean wasn't walking along the bank this way, and then I realized that it was now or never; I couldn't stay here much longer or I'd drown. I grasped the salt grass blades in both hands and started to pull, but my hands let go as soon as the pain hit. It felt like my palms were being sawed in two. I sank for a few seconds and almost panicked. Then I was up and breathing again and tearing at the buttons of my shirt. I ripped it open and struggled with the sleeves, then I got it off and wrapped my worst hand tightly in the wet cloth. I bundled a thick bunch of grass blades with my other hand and carefully placed them in the grasp of the bandaged one, then grabbed another handful in the unprotected hand, let myself sink to the length of my arms, gave a strong kick with my legs, and heaved with all the strength I had left.

It was enough, almost. I got my body nearly to the waist onto the bank and then started slipping slowly backward. I thrashed and squirmed and struggled, and then my right leg was up, knee on the bank and lodged behind a clump of salt grass, and I levered myself up into the rain and the wonderful, pounding wind that I could breathe. I lay gasping. It was not safety, but it wasn't death by drowning, either. After a minute I raised my head and looked for Dean. He was still standing where

I'd last seen him, but as I looked, he started to pace the bank, moving a few feet in one direction and then a few feet in the other, toward me and then away. As he turned toward me, I ducked into the grass, and when he didn't come for me, I cautiously raised up again and saw him just pacing up and down. He was looking out at the water and swinging the pipe back and forth in his hand. When he turned away this time, I started crawling on my belly toward the shed.

"Milam, you bitch!"

I froze. I wasn't sure I'd even heard it in the roar of the wind. Then it came again. "You bitch, you goddamned bitch! I *wanted* to kill you! I wanted to! I wanted to!" The voice was a howl amid the howl of the storm, but the words were clear enough. He'd said, "I wanted to kill you." Past tense. Dean Caney thought I was dead.

I almost sobbed when the realization hit. All I'd have to do was stay low, stay on my belly in the cover of the grass, and when I got a chance, get to that shed or into those bushes. He'd leave, and I'd ride out the storm, and the nightmare would be over. Then he yelled again, and what he yelled was, "Milam, I'm gonna kill that fucking Judy, too."

CHAPTER 26

Scuttling and slithering on my belly through the mud and the stiff clumps of salt grass, I got to the little shed at last and lay gasping, blessedly out of the wind. I lay for I don't know how long, maybe five minutes, I guess. I had no will to do anything else, and no strength or breath left in my body. But I was alive, and I could hardly believe how wonderful it was. After a while, my breathing steadied and I started thinking again. My first thought was of getting back to my truck, and my second thought was of what Dean had said, or I thought he'd said: "I'm going to kill Judy, too."

Surely he couldn't have said that. If he'd wanted to kill her, he'd have done it last night when he went to her house, wouldn't he? Of course he would. But what if he really meant it? He'd killed Sandy and he'd killed that poor guy he stole the Jeep from, and if he hadn't killed me, it hadn't been from lack of trying. I was about half killed, anyway. I had to believe him, to assume he was telling the truth about going to kill Judy. And if he was, maybe her only chance was for me to get to her first. I tottered groaning to my feet and looked around the corner of the shed.

The wind-driven rain slammed into my face full-force and blinded me for a few seconds until I got a hand up to shield my eyes and peered out under my fingers. I looked and looked, but I didn't see Dean. Slowly I eased around the corner, forcing myself forward into the wind, keeping as close as possible to the wall of the shed. The boards of the wall were rough with splinters and peeling paint, and my bare upper body scraped painfully against it as I inched along. I'd lost my damn shirt somewhere out in the salt grass. The rain peppered my exposed skin like millions of BBs. I got to the front corner of the shed and looked around it. No Dean.

The shed had double doors with a padlock and hasp joining them, but the wind had worked them until I could see that the staple of the hasp was barely hanging into the wood by its screws. If this was a maintenance shed for the cemetery, maybe I could get a shovel or something to use for a weapon. At least maybe I could make Dean think I could hurt him. If I went after him unarmed, I was signing my own death warrant, and that wasn't going to do Judy any good, either. I got hold of the padlock and gave it a hard yank.

The pain from my injured hand was like a red explosion in my head. I screamed and reeled against the shed doors. I don't think it could have hurt any more to have the hand cut off. The salt grass blades had really done a job on it. When I could, I took off my belt with my left hand and looped it behind the loosened hasp. Then, still holding with only my left hand, I leaned back and pulled. The screws pulled right out of the wood and I staggered backwards with the sudden release. I didn't fall only because the force of the wind didn't let me. I buckled the belt back around my waist without trying to run it through my belt loops and pulled the door open enough against the monstrous wind to squeeze inside.

The door slammed behind me, and I was in pitch darkness. I was between the door and something big and metallic that was so familiar that even the calves of my legs recognized it from pressing against it. It was the grill of an old Ford tractor. The feel of it there in the alien dark was like coming home. I thought of my old 9N Ford on its trailer in my garage on Hank Street, and I wanted to be home more than anything in the world. Home, safe, and dry. Warm, out of the wind and the water, naked between clean, smooth sheets, feeling the gentle breeze the attic fan drew across my bed, listening to the breeze in the neighbors' cottonwood rustling like rain, and dreaming of warm and lovely Lisa. I shook my head, wiped water from my face with my left hand, and went groping in the roaring darkness for a shovel.

I found absolutely nothing in the shed I could use for a weapon. You'd think a graveyard would have a shovel around, at least. But no, nothing. There was a lawnmower and some cans I took to be gas cans and some quart cans of oil for the mower and tractor and a pile of shop rags, all of which I recognized by feel, but no hand tools at all, not even a wrench. The tractor had no tool box on it that I could find, either. I supposed whoever worked here brought all their tools with them, probably somebody like me who maintained a lot of places and just kept the cemetery's own stuff here. I felt my way back to the door and pushed outside by leaning on it with all my weight against the wind. I'd just have to take the truck—and now that I thought about it, I had a tire tool in there that would be a match for Dean's piece of pipe, and some wrenches, too, of course—and get to Judy's if I could in all this weather. I made my way around the tractor shed and looked down the little road that ran through the gate of the cemetery where I'd left my truck. The truck was gone.

I almost despaired, then. My truck is like a part of my body to me. It's more than just a piece of transportation. It's my mobility and my means of livelihood and a part of my self-image as a dyke, a landscaper, and an independent human being. I howled with rage when I realized Dean Caney had taken it, and with despair when I thought of how long it would take me to get through the storm on foot the mile or so to Judy's house, where no doubt Dean was already arriving. I'd be too late to save Judy, just like I'd been too late for Claudia. I cursed myself for a coward and a fool and a brainless idiot that never thought of anything to do until the time for it was long gone. Then I got hold of myself and molded that anger down into a white-hot, burning core of determination not to give up unless I knew for a fact that it was over and Dean had won. Maybe he hadn't gotten to Judy's. Maybe if he had, he hadn't gotten into the house. Maybe she'd had a gun and shot him. Or even if he'd already killed her, maybe he hadn't gotten away yet. If I had anything to do with it, he wasn't ever going to get away. That lovely old Ford tractor was going to take me to him.

I wrenched the shed doors open and the wind snatched them away from me and tore one of them off its hinges and tumbled it away into the dark. The tractor, I'd noticed before, didn't have any kind of mower hooked up to it, which was fine with me, but I wondered what use anybody made of it out here if it wasn't for mowing. I didn't care, right now.

I reached for the steering wheel and knew right away that I wasn't going to be able even to haul myself up there, much less steer the thing in a hurricane, without getting something to protect my torn hand. I groped around in the back of the shed where I'd felt what I presumed were shop rags before and found a pile of them. They were wet, of course — the wind was forcing water through every crack and opening in the shed like spray from a high-pressure hose — but a couple in the middle of the pile weren't too bad, and I didn't feel any grease or stiffness in them. I used my teeth and my left hand and tied one rag around my right palm as well as I could, and then I used my right hand and my teeth to do the same for the left. The left hand wasn't too bad just from pulling myself out of the canal by the salt grass blades, but I figured it was in for a rough time, too. I caught hold of the steering wheel again and climbed onto the tractor, first missing my footing and banging my shin hard. The thing didn't have the little running board footrests that mine did. I felt with my hand and found only an iron peg set too far forward to make getting up into the seat very easy if you weren't used to it. This must be a really old machine. I got my foot on the peg, crouched, and lunged awkwardly up and into the seat. Now to start it. I felt around the dashboard for the key, and there wasn't one.

The ignition switch with its empty keyhole was right there beneath my fingers where it should have been. But some of these old tractors had been modified over the years and the original switch bypassed. I kept feeling carefully over the instrument panel, and there, sure enough, was a little toggle switch where nothing ought to be. I flipped it. I was afraid it would just turn the lights on or something, but nothing happened, so that must be the ignition switch, all right — or else it was for the lights and the battery was dead. I checked the shift lever to be sure it was in neutral, wiggled the throttle a little, pulled out the choke, and hit the starter on the transmission case with my toe. Absolutely nothing happened. I yelled with frustration, picturing Dean Caney in my truck racing toward Judy's with his piece of pipe on the seat beside him. I fumbled around the instrument panel some more and finally my fingers touched some kind of button. I pushed it, and the wonderful machine's engine turned over fast a couple of times, caught and roared like a race car. I adjusted the throttle and let it warm up, and then I put the transmission in gear and eased forward into the hurricane.

I found out right off that this wasn't going to be a picnic like my Saturday mowing jobs were generally. I was glad for the little footpegs, because they seemed to have turned-up ends that kept my feet from sliding off, and I was half-standing and riding the old machine like a horse, trying to keep it going where I wanted it to in the wind and slippery mud. This tractor did have lights, I was glad to see, so I could see a little of where I was going, at least for a few feet in front of me. I resolved to put lights on my own tractor when I got home.

I got down to the cemetery gate all right, and it was open and half torn off its hinges. I went through, passed the place where I'd left my truck, and saw ruts in the mud where Dean had come close to getting stuck when he stole it. I wished to god he had, because I could have chased him down and killed him right there. I was going to kill him if I could, even if it meant I spent the next twenty years on stud row at the Texas Department of Corrections. I wrestled the tractor onto the shell-paved road, crosswise to the wind, and headed for Judy's.

It was a wild ride. I was pushing the old tractor as fast as I could and still not bounce too much to stay on the road. Every now and then there'd be something in the road I had to go over or around, like pieces of corrugated iron off a roof somewhere, a piece of a door, a gate, or some other wreckage. If there'd been trees along here, I knew some of them would have been down across the road. And sure enough, when I did get to a part with some trees, a big one was down, the road was mostly blocked, and there was my beautiful truck sitting skewed across the road with its rear wheels in a water-filled ditch.

I steered the tractor around the lashing limbs of the top of the tree and kept on for Judy's, now looking all the time for Dean on foot. The last thing I wanted was to have him suddenly loom up out of the night beside the road and drag me off my tractor. I stood up so I'd be too tall for him to hit in the head from the ground and paid attention. Once I saw a movement out of the corner of my eye and nearly had a heart attack, but it was a poor cow, standing with her head down and her legs splayed to keep her on her feet. I hollered, "Hang in there, Bossy!" and went on by.

There were no lights at Judy's house and I almost missed it. All the trees looked different, and it was hard to see the roadway at all. I guessed the power was out on account of the storm, because I didn't see any lights anywhere and this was right up close to the town of Port Bolivar itself. I guided the tractor over a washed-out place full of running water at the end of Judy's driveway and nearly bounced off the seat as I took it too fast. But I stayed aboard and gunned the machine up the drive toward the house. I was looking to see if the door looked like it had been broken into or anything, but I couldn't see a thing in the dark except the general outlines of the place and the darker rectangles where the doors and windows were. And then the next thing I knew, something hit me in the ribs like a pile driver and I was flying through the air. I hit the ground by the righthand side of the tractor and yanked my feet back to keep from being run over. It just missed me with its big back wheel as it rolled on by without me.

I thought a flying tree limb must have got me. Judging from the ones I'd seen lying on the road, that seemed likely. I was wrong, though. Dean Caney was dashing for Judy's front door, and I saw him get there and start bashing at it with his piece of pipe. The door was a hollow core job and it started to splinter and give right away. He was going to get in and kill Judy while I lay here in the mud. It was too soon to feel much pain yet from the force of the blow, but he'd really cracked my ribs a good one. Now I was down and he was making short work of the barrier between him and Judy, and I wasn't going to be able to do anything about it.

Oh, yes I was, too. I'd had it with this son-of-a-bitch. I got up and braced against a tree and yelled, "Hey, Caney" at the top of my lungs.

I didn't know whether or not he'd hear me over the wind, but he did. He turned and instantly started for me with his pipe ready. Of course I hadn't had enough sense to stop at my truck and get a wrench or a tire tool for defense. Good work, Milam. I put my head down and ran right at him.

I guess my attack must have thrown him a little, because instead of swinging his pipe and clubbing me like a cow at the slaughterhouse, he tried to step aside. I hit him a glancing blow with my head, he lurched backward under the impact, and we went down in a tangle of arms and legs.

The side where he'd hit me was beginning to hurt a lot, but I was fighting for my life. I grabbed the hand that had the pipe in it. He thrashed and swore. He was amazingly strong, but I hung on, and by sheer good luck

I got his wrist in front of my mouth and bit the hell out of it. I didn't let go, either, but held on like a snapping turtle and sank my teeth into the tendons of his tough, old wrist right to the bone.

Dean screamed like a wounded rabbit, desperate and shrill in my ear, and the hand dropped the pipe. He was tearing my hair out of my head with his other hand, trying to pull me loose, bending my head right back until I thought my neck would snap, but I locked my jaws and held on. He dragged me up on my feet, beating on my back and shoulders and screaming all the time. It must have only taken a few seconds altogether, but I remember having plenty of time to hope he wasn't going to hit me in the ribs again, or I knew I'd black out. He didn't have a chance to think of it, though, because while I still had his wrist in my teeth, there was a tremendous crack, louder even than the storm, and something enormous loomed suddenly over our heads and came down on us like a falling mountain.

I'd been stunned, I realized, and was lying pinned to the ground by an almost unbearable, crushing weight. Dean was there, too, not moving. My teeth were still clamped in his wrist, and I could taste a lot of blood. I had to make an effort to unclench my jaw muscles and let him go, and when I did, his hand dropped limply in the mud. I couldn't tell if he was breathing or not, but I was, and every breath hurt like hell. I tried to move, but the rough-barked, big live oak that had fallen on us just didn't give at all. I thought it was going to take a tractor to pull this tree off of us, and I'd probably wrecked mine. Anyway, who was going to drive it?

I must have passed out for a little while, because the next thing I knew, most of the rain and the noise of the storm had died away and it was grey daylight. Dean was moaning, short little semiconscious moans like a person coming out from under an anesthetic. Judy's voice was repeating frantically, "Cass! Cass! Are you all right? Cass!" Her hand was shaking my shoulder.

"Judy, kill this bastard," I said, and passed out again.

Later, I heard the ear-splitting noise of a chain saw very close and felt the tree trunk shift over my ribs, making me scream. Still later, the horrible weight was off of me and I was lying on my back in the soaking wet grass with Judy on her knees over me, wiping my face with a cloth and crying.

"Did you kill him?" I said.

"No. I think he's dying, anyway. Oh, Cass."

I struggled to sit up, gasped with pain, and lay back. "You better tie him up or something," I told her between clenched teeth. "He was gonna kill you, too."

"Can you get into the house, Cass?"

I moved very cautiously, got onto my knees, and Judy helped me up. I could walk, all right, with her support; it was just that it hurt like hell. I was a little dizzy, too. She got me down on her couch, and I closed my eyes and tried to think of what ought to be done right now.

"Does your phone work?" I asked her.

"No. And the power's off, too."

"Have you got anything I could drink, like some milk or something? I think I'll be okay when I get something in my stomach."

"Sure." She went and got me a glass of milk and a piece of some kind of coffee cake and I didn't have any trouble getting it down, though my teeth were real sore from biting Dean. After I'd had the food, I felt better.

Judy had gone back outside, and when she came back I was ready to get up if I could. I pushed myself onto my feet and found that if I moved very carefully, I could get around a little.

"What about Dean?" I asked.

"Still the same, I think. I don't know how we're going to get help for him. I've been to all the neighbors', but I guess everybody but me evacuated before the storm got too bad. I should have listened to the radio. I'm sorry, Cass."

"Yeah, well. Is he conscious?"

162

"A little. I think he's out of his head."

"Babe," I said, "you can say that again." I crept carefully out the door and squelched slowly through the yard to the remains of the tree and the remains of Dean Caney. Judy had gotten the branch off of him and laid him out on his back with a pillow under his head and covered him with a couple of blankets. He looked grey under his tan, but he was breathing.

"Caney," I said. "Why did you kill Sandy?"

He moaned, and his eyelids fluttered, but that's all.

"Dean," I tried again. "Talk to me. It'll be better."

He opened his eyes and squinted up at me. "Marilyn?" he said.

"Cass Milam, Dean. Why'd you kill Sandy Marigold?"

"You goddamn dykes." His voice was low and strained. I got painfully down on my knees and leaned over him to hear him. "Oh, Marilyn." He closed his eyes again and lay there breathing, breathing. I watched the shallow rise and fall of his chest. There was something badly wrong with it; the motion sort of rippled and bumped up on one side, leaving a hollow-looking place on the other. He'd gotten the worst of the falling tree. Chances were, he'd taken most of the weight and saved me.

"Dean," I said, "tell me why you did it. Tell me."

He didn't open his eyes, and for a minute I thought he wasn't going to answer. Then he almost whispered, his voice was so soft, and I put my ear close to his lips to hear the words. "I tried so hard."

I waited for more. When it didn't come, I said, "Tried hard to what, Dean?"

"Not hate Marilyn."

"But you loved her, didn't you?"

"Goddamned dyke. She never cared at all."

He was silent. So was I. I wanted to say something, but I didn't know what. So Dean had hung around lesbians all this time because he was trying not to hate his old love for being one of us. Hate and hurt had beaten him in the end. Sandy and the guy at Cat Mountain had died for it, and Judy and I nearly had, and I thought Dean was as good as dead, too. "She probably cared, Dean," I said.

"She's dead, anyway."

I thought of Claudia's grave. "Yes," I said.

Judy came out with another blanket and we covered him with it, too. She said, "I wish we could get him in the house."

"We'd just hurt him. Anyway, I don't think I could help carry him. I think I've got broken ribs."

Judy brought out two chairs and set them down near where Dean was lying, and we sat there with him. At long last we heard a motor, and then a four-wheel-drive truck came into sight on the road, and Judy ran out and flagged it down. Two men from the Port Bolivar Volunteer Fire Department were in it, and they took over with Dean. They checked him out and looked grim, and I noticed one of them looking thoughtfully at the wrist I'd mutilated. Judy had bandaged it, but the fireman had unwrapped it and now he frowned at it before wrapping it in a clean bandage. Even from where I stood, it was obvious that the wounds in it were tooth marks. One of the firemen ran back to the truck, and I could see him talking into a microphone. CB, I realized. Good. I told Judy, "Go tell him to get the cops out here."

She did, and I sat in the chair and closed my eyes. I kept dozing off, and whenever I would, I'd start to lean over and the ribs would stab me awake again. I barely remember Judy's helping me up and guiding me into the house. She turned back the covers on a smooth, clean bed, and I eased my filthy, battered body into it and dropped into dreamless sleep.

CHAPTER 27

It was nearly noon when I finally opened my eyes again. Judy, or at least I hoped it was Judy, had managed to get my clothes off of me and sponge off a good bit of the mud and blood. I drew the sheet carefully aside and raised my head to stare at my abused body. I had a lot of scrapes and little cuts, and there were going to be some really spectacular bruises. I had a throbbing pain in my left shoulder that I couldn't remember when I'd got, and my hands were bandaged in what looked like strips of flower-print sheets. I wondered if Judy had destroyed a good sheet to fix me up. It was my ribs that really hurt when I tried to move, though. I didn't see how I was going to get out of bed at all. Maybe if I kept my body perfectly straight. . . . I worked carefully and got my legs over the side of the bed and sat up. Judy heard me yell as I did it and came hurrying in.

"Cass! You shouldn't be out of bed!" I think she would have pushed me back down, but she was afraid to hurt me. She stood there sort of fluttering her hands.

"If I don't get out of it, I'm going to pee in it. Help me to the jane, Judy." I gave her a smile.

She did, and walking wasn't as bad as I'd been afraid it might be. Judy's arm steadied me, but I could have made it on my own. Good. A couple of aspirin ought to have me back in working order.

When I got out of the bathroom, Judy wanted me back in bed, but I was ravenously hungry and made her let me go into the kitchen. She helped me wrap a robe around myself and tied the sash for me so I wouldn't have to fumble for it with my bandaged, stiff hands, and I sat down at her kitchen table while she cooked me bacon and eggs. The smell made my mouth water so much I had to keep swallowing.

While she cooked, she filled me in on what I'd missed.

An ambulance had come for Dean, but they hadn't been able to get up the street because of debris in the roadway, so they'd ended up carrying him off on a stretcher, two men carrying the stretcher while two more walked alongside, one holding up the IV bottle and the other holding the tube and needle in Dean's arm. They didn't look too hopeful, Judy told me.

The sheriff had come as the ambulance was leaving, but Judy didn't know much to tell him beyond what I'd told her last night before the storm and what she'd found in her yard this morning. She'd been in the kitchen in the back of the house and never even heard Dean beating down her front door, or if she had, she'd just attributed it to storm noise, which she was trying not to think about too much. The downed oak with the two bodies pinned under it was a complete surprise to her when she'd come out at dawn to check for damage. It was the sheriff who had pointed out to her that the damage to her front door might have been done by the length of pipe he found lying a few feet from where she'd found me and Dean.

I was surprised the sheriff hadn't insisted on waking me up to tell him about it, but Judy said the law down here had its hands full right now trying to get things back in working order and coordinate the cleanup. She'd heard that the damage hadn't been too bad most places. Apparently the hurricane had swooped down the coast and come in right across Galveston. She'd turned out her lights and gone to bed right after I'd left, having gulped a few slugs of bourbon to steady her nerves after my visit, and never heard that everybody was supposed to evacuate the area. Her neighbors and the civil defense people

166

that went around notifying stragglers to get out must have thought she'd already gone. The storm had woken her up, but even though it sounded like the howling hounds of hell, she relied on what she'd heard on earlier reports and assumed it wasn't really as bad as it sounded.

"So I got up and made coffee and sat in the kitchen so I'd be away from those front windows in case the wind blew them in, and spent the rest of the night thinking about you and Claudia and wondering if Jack, who's kind of scatterbrained, had heard about the storm and was concerned enough to cut his business trip short and try to come home. I couldn't call him, because the phone was out."

She put a cup of coffee in front of me, and a big plate of bacon and scrambled eggs. "I want you to eat all you can, Cass, because I'm having to cook everything in the refrigerator now, and if the power stays off much longer, I'll have to open the freezer and start on things in there, I guess. So keep putting it away, will you?"

I said I'd give it my best shot. Then, "Judy, did Dean ever say anything else? Did he talk at all?"

"No, not that I heard. The ambulance men might have heard something, I don't know. What was he trying to do, anyway? Did he really beat my door down like that?"

"Yep, he did, and he said he was going to kill you. He was going to kill all us 'goddamned dykes.' "

Judy flinched a little at the word, 'dykes.' I said, "That's a perfectly good word, Judy, when we use it."

She shuddered. "It's just so. . . ." She turned from the stove and smiled apologetically.

"It's a strong word for strong women, babe." I grinned at her discomfort. "And speaking of which, where'd you ever learn to use a chain saw like that? That was a hell of a tree to cut up without cutting us up, too."

It was her turn to grin. "I'm not such a weak sister, babe." We laughed. It hurt my ribs.

When she saw me wince, Judy at once became all motherly concern. "You need to get to a doctor, Cass.

You ought to have X-rays. You might be hurt worse than you think."

"Well, I'll do that when I get home, if I'm not any better. Okay?"

"You ought to do it here. You'll stay a few days, at least, won't you?"

I thought of my truck in the ditch and my bashed and aching body, and I thought of my quiet, peaceful, safe house on Hank Street, and I thought of my lovely dyke friends who would have heard about the hurricane and be worried about me by now, and I thought of how glad Lisa would be to see me. Maybe she'd stay with me at my house for a little while, just until I got over the worst of this. Maybe that would be real, real nice. Maybe.

"I'm getting out of here as fast as I can get my truck on the road," I told Judy. "But first, I want some more of whatever you're cooking, and I want some to take with me, and I want about two more cups of your good coffee." She shook her head and sighed. "And I want to thank you, Judy. For taking care of Claudia and all. I wish I could have helped. I guess if she'd wanted me, though, she would have called me."

Judy came over and put her hands on my shoulders. "She loved you, Cass. I used to wonder if she regretted leaving you for me. But you know how she was. She'd never have admitted it."

"She had her pride." I reached up and put my bandaged hand over Judy's. "What happened to my tractor?"

She squeezed my shoulders and freed her hand and turned back to her cooking. "I found it up against the garage door, still running, like it wanted to get in. I turned it off. There was just that little switch to flip, or at least I hope that's all I needed to do."

"Right, that's it. Was it wrecked, the front end or anything?"

"I didn't notice. Why?"

"Because if you're that good with a chain saw, you ought to be able to drive a tractor, too, and I need it to pull my truck back on the road. I really don't think my ribs are ready for a tractor ride just yet."

She turned off the burners under three pans and handed me the clothes she'd been drying over a chair in front of the oven. She helped me get them on and gave me a clean, soft tee shirt that must have been Jack's. Then we went out to see about the tractor.

It was smack up against the garage door, like Judy had said, and the grill and the door were a little damaged. Other than that, it seemed to be in miraculously good order. I was seeing it in the light for the first time, and it was indeed an old Ford Ferguson, probably one of the very early ones. It had some rust showing through the grey paint here and there, and those modifications had been made to the ignition switch and the starter, but other than that it looked like it was all original. I was glad I hadn't wrecked it.

I helped Judy up by coaching from the ground and showed her how all the controls worked. After she had the clutch, brake, gearshift, and throttle down, I told her how to start it, and the engine came to life in that good old even, Ford idle that I loved to hear. She backed the tractor up and turned, keeping it under careful control, and started for the place where Dean had left my truck. I walked slowly along behind her, and by the time I'd gotten there, she had the tractor already in position to pull and had even found my tow chain in my tool box and had hooked it up.

"Damn good work!" I told her.

"I told you I wasn't a weak sister."

"No kidding." With me giving advice, Judy eased the tractor forward, the old engine got down and took up the strain, and the truck followed her up out of the ditch like a puppy on a leash. I had her stop while I got laboriously into the cab and tried the starter. I didn't know what to expect after the storm, but my lovely Chevy started just like it was in my driveway at home. I let it idle while I helped Judy, or really mostly just encouraged her, to unhook the tow chain and stow it back in the

169

tool box. Then I climbed painfully up into the truck again, knocked the engine off the choke, and we drove carefully around the fallen tree and back to Judy's.

There was a Galveston County sheriff's car in Judy's driveway, and another car, too. I saw Sergeants Alcorn and Harris following the Galveston deputies around the corner from the back of the house. I sighed.

The ordeal of the police wasn't too bad, though. We sat around the kitchen table with coffee, and I went over the events of the last two days in response to their questions. I gave them all the details I could remember, though I was sure I'd think of more later, probably for weeks to come. A lot had been happening, and none of it had been very pleasant.

They had a hard time understanding why I'd even come to Galveston in the first place and mixed myself up in a "police matter," and I wasn't feeling like apologizing for getting down here in time to maybe save Judy's life. They wanted to know exactly where I'd been and who I'd talked to, and they weren't impressed, either, by my rather lame-sounding explanation of why I'd spent the night at the cemetery in my truck. I wasn't about to try to tell them about that part of it; I had no desire to cry in front of all these cops.

They finally gave up on me and told me the news: Dean Caney had died on the way to Galveston. He'd had massive internal injuries from the falling tree. I must have just lucked out.

They weren't too happy with what I'd told them about what Caney's motive for all this murder and mayhem seemed to be, the stuff about his old girlfriend. I think the idea of any man's caring about any dyke was beyond them. They could probably understand the killing, but not the caring. "Well," Alcorn said, "I guess we'll have to go with that. We didn't find anything else to explain it. There was nothing in his house or office or the Jeep he stole."

"Where was the Jeep?"

"Right down the road about half a mile from the cemetery."

"Huh. But where was Caney all the time between when he talked to Judy and when he came after me?"

The Galveston deputies shifted in their seats and looked at each other, and Harris started curling the page of his notebook between his finger and thumb. "Fishing," Alcorn said.

"Fishing?"

"That's right. He got busted for fishing without a license, right by the ferry slip yesterday evening. But of course nobody checked the APB we had out on him, so all he got was a ticket. Now, this is only a theory, but what we think is, he must have been waiting around here trying to decided what to do next. He probably hadn't decided to kill Judy by then. You can get lost in a crowd of fishermen down there when there's a good run on, and he really couldn't have picked a better place to hide, except that he didn't have a fishing license. Of course" —and he shot a look at the uncomfortable deputies —"that didn't do him any harm, did it? He didn't even have to pay the ticket."

"So why did he change his mind about Judy, then?"

"Of course this is—"

"Only a theory, right."

"Only a guess, but we think he probably saw you getting off the ferry. If he did, he'd check you out and think over what to do, and the rest you know."

"Yeah."

"What we don't know is why he didn't just shoot you. He had a .357 magnum in his belt when they got him to the morgue."

171

CHAPTER 28

Judy packed me a lunch and a thermos of black coffee to go with it, I hugged her as well as I could without flinching and kissed her goodbye. I don't usually kiss straight women, but I made an exception.

"Be careful, Cass," she said, and I said I would. I got in the truck and started the engine, and Judy said, "Keep in touch."

"I will," I said.

I could see her standing there in the driveway until I turned the corner and a house cut off my view.

It was nearly four o'clock and I just wanted to get home. The ferry was running all right, and there was hardly any line for it at all. I just drove right onto the boat like I did it all the time, and when I'd set my brakes and turned the engine off, I got out carefully and looked in the water can mounted behind the cab to check on my beer. The four cans of Schlitz were still there, and I fished them all out and put them on the seat. They were even still kind of cold. I opened one and sipped it as I sat in the truck and let the Cone Johnson, the name I'd noticed on the front of this boat, take me back to Galveston. I figured I had about a five-hour trip back to Austin. I hurt, and I felt kind of dead and empty inside, drained out. I couldn't stand to think of Sandy dead, and that poor guy with the Jeep and his wife and kids, and Claudia lying in the Port Bolivar graveyard, lost forever.

Then I concentrated on driving and finding my way to the road back to Houston. I forced myself to look at the storm damage, which really only showed up in a few places to me, like where there were traffic lights down or a roof damaged here and there. I guess it hadn't really been a bad storm. There were a lot of power lines down, though, and I didn't see any lights anywhere, traffic signals or anything. When I got to a gas station on Broadway, I stopped and tried the pay phone, but it was dead as a hammer. Judy had been right about all the phones being out. I got back in the truck and got rolling.

I'd really wanted to call Lisa or Jacko. I knew they'd be worried. I knew Jacko would be, at least. So much had happened in the last two days, I'd been back in the past so much, that Lisa seemed almost like a dream to me. I felt like I'd been gone a year from the time she kissed me goodbye, only yesterday morning. I wouldn't have been surprised to get back to Austin and find her completely different from the Lisa in my mind. And there was always Sharla, too. Maybe she'd got her hooks into Lisa while I was gone. I wished I could call Lisa and at least warn her I was coming back. I had a sick feeling I might walk in and find her in Sharla's arms. I made up my mind to stop in Houston, where the phones would surely be working, and call Jacko. She'd get hold of Lisa for me. I suddenly felt too shy even to call Lisa myself.

Once I got out of Galveston and over the causeway bridge onto the mainland, the Gulf Freeway was littered with debris that I had to watch out for to avoid running over. I was glad it wasn't dark yet.

I got to a place where there were barricades up and "two-way traffic" signs, and the whole southbound side of the freeway was closed by a gigantic pile of timbers and seaweed and I don't know what all that the Highway Department hadn't had time to pick up. It was going to take a bulldozer to clear and a bunch of trucks to haul it off. I slowed down and kept in the right lane while, on the other side of the row of orange cones that had been set out, a thin string of traffic heading for Galveston crept along. I wondered if these were people who'd run from the storm and were coming home. If they were, I hoped they'd find their houses and their animals safe tonight. There was an ice truck with the name of a Houston company on it. I'll bet they'll be glad to see that, I thought. I thought of Judy cooking all the food from her refrigerator and freezer and waiting for the power to come back on so she could save it. She could use some of that ice. And maybe her husband Jack was in one of these cars. I hoped she wouldn't have to spend tonight alone, even if it meant she had to spend it with him. A brown Honda went by, an older black Chevy, a Ford pickup with a shell camper on it, a silver Toyota. The Toyota had several people in it, a blonde woman driving.

I did a double take, but the Toyota was past me without my being able to get a look at the other passengers in it. I took my foot off the gas. It couldn't have been Lisa's car, could it? I searched my rear view mirror, and I saw brake lights back down the road. It couldn't be, but I flashed my brake lights at the guy behind me and pulled off onto the shoulder and stopped. I watched the mirror, and, sure enough, the Toyota was making a U-turn. I sat in the truck and waited, and Lisa's car pulled up and stopped behind me, and Lisa and Jacko and Kelley and Elkhorn all started piling out. I climbed out to meet them.

Elkhorn, who'd been driving, got to me first and grabbed me. I yelled, "Wait! Careful!" and she backed off, and then the others were there and everybody was laughing and talking at once, and I saw Lisa kind of hanging back, and I just went over and stood in front of her, not paying attention to anybody else. I found I couldn't even speak. I just stood there and looked at her. I could see tears in her eyes, and there were some in mine, too. The Gulf breeze ruffled her beautiful, dark hair, and I reached out for her slowly and took hold of her arms. "I think my ribs are broken, babe," I said. And then we both started talking and bawling at once, saying, "I missed you," and "I was so worried," and a bunch of other stuff like that, and Jacko and Kelley and Elkhorn crowded around asking questions and talking about how they'd decided to come rescue me from the hurricane.

Everybody agreed I shouldn't drive in my condition, so Lisa and I got in my truck with Elkhorn behind the wheel, while Kelley and Jacko went back to Lisa's car and brought us a six-pack of Shiner, ice cold. "We thought you might need this, lady," Jacko said, and she climbed halfway across Lisa and kissed me. Then we started for Austin, me with a Shiner in my bandaged hand and no reason not to drink while Elkhorn drove, enjoying driving a truck for a change. Lisa sat beside me and kept touching me in little, loving ways that told me I never should have worried about going home to her.

After a few minutes or so of general conversation, Lisa took an envelope out of her pocket and handed it to me. "This came in your mail," she said.

I looked at the return address. Department of Public Safety, Records Division. "I know what it says," I said, and I folded it and put it in my pocket.

"So, Milam, what happened? Did you have a fight, or get caught in the storm, or what? What kind of war were you in?" Elkhorn said.

I took Lisa's hand in mine and then reached over and put my other one on Elkhorn's bony knee.

"I'll tell you all about it," I said.

Books From Banned Books

Kite Music,
Gary Shellhart $8.95

Mountain Climbing in Sheridan Square,
Stan Leventhal $8.95

Skiptrace,
Antoinette Azolakov $8.95

A Cry in the Desert,
Jed A. Bryan $9.95

Cass and the Stone Butch,
Antoinette Azolakov $8.95

Dreams of the Woman Who Loved Sex,
Tee Corinne $7.95

Tangled Sheets,
Gerard Curry $7.95

Death Strip,
Benita Kirkland $8.95

Days in the Sun,
Drew Kent $8.95

Fairy Tales Mother Never Told You,
Benjamin Eakin $5.95

These books are available from your favorite bookstore or directly from:

BANNED BOOKS
Number 231, P.O. Box 33280, Austin, Texas 78704

Add 15% of order total for postage and handling. Texas residents, please add 8% sales tax.